Dear Reader:

We begin September with the return of a much-loved writer. In *Where Enchantment Lies* (#358), Beth Brookes explores a controversial subject in a powerfully poignant love story. Journalist Taylor Grant can hardly believe his eyes. Katie Riordan has cured a heart attack victim simply by touching him! Is she a clever fake or a walking miracle? In his pursuit of the answer, he's captivated by Katie's magical warmth ... her frightening vulnerability. Like a blazing sunbeam, she transforms his cynicism into hope and heals his battered heart. Whether or not you "believe" in Katie's special power, you'll be mesmerized by an author who clearly has a special touch...

Carole Buck's popularity continues to soar, and *Cody's Honor* (#359) is sure to keep her flying. Widow Geneva Butler, locked in the bathroom by her two-year-old daughter, is rescued by dashing Cody Merrill, the man she's unconsciously desired since the day he served as best man at her wedding! When little Ammie accidentally pulls off Geneva's towel, the attraction both Geneva and Cody have secretly repressed flares into white-hot passion ... But Cody, intent on doing the "honorable" thing, is convinced an affair is impossible, marriage unthinkable ... The path to their "happily ever after" may be roundabout, but it provides romantic entertainment of the highest order, every step of the way.

This month two terrific new writers make stunning debuts. The first, Molly Thomas, is bound to win instant popularity with *Rebel Heart* (#360). Ginger Malone's temper has landed her in jail! And now big, macho cowboy Mack Walker is paying her bail—and forcing her to stay at his ranch! Mack's a hero in the classic mold—with the sensitivity to calm Ginger's terrors, the passion to fire her longings. Ginger's a spitfire whose tough words hide secret pain, whose womanly needs have been too long denied. *Rebel Heart* positively crackles with energy and excitement!

Then, take a deep breath and plunge into the heady sensuality of *Dark Splendor* (#361). Liz Grady brings us another deeply moving love story, this time pairing a man and woman who don't know how lost they've been until they find each other. Social opposites, surly cab driver Ben Lucas and chic dating consultant Jill Maxwell must struggle with pride and prejudice, must overcome deep-seated grief and insidious suspicions, before concluding that true love *does* conquer all. Another beauty from the incomparable Liz Grady.

Our second new writer this month, Samantha Quinn, tackles an intriguing situation in *Forever Kate* (#362), in which Katharine Drake, who's been married twice, is now engaged to a third—wrong—man! Then Nicky Lockwood, the boy next door with whom she shared the triumphs and tragedies of growing up, steps back into her life. Now a mature, virile man, he's the *only* guy who can obliterate the formal, reserved person she's become, coaxing forth the fun-loving Kate she was meant to be. *Forever Kate,* warm and lighthearted, will leave you supremely satisfied—and asking for more.

Finally, sparkling with Frances Davies's distinctive wit and a mile-wide streak of romanticism, *Fortune's Hunter* (#363) returns us to the picturesque English village that set the stage for the rollicking *Fortune's Darling* (#296). Those who savored that deftly original story will view it from a totally new perspective in this clever tour de force. Those entering Thrum for the first time will revel in the ardent reunion of two lovers who've pined for each other for over a decade ... But there's one slight problem: The hero doesn't recognize his long-lost heartthrob! A funny, heartwarming romp, complete with an infuriating yew maze, an ornery goose, and one woman's oh, so sweet revenge.

Enjoy! and warm wishes,

Ellen Edwards

Ellen Edwards, Senior Editor
SECOND CHANCE AT LOVE
The Berkley Publishing Group
200 Madison Avenue
New York, NY 10016

SECOND CHANCE AT LOVE™

BETH BROOKES
WHERE ENCHANTMENT LIES

A
SECOND CHANCE AT LOVE
BOOK

Second Chance at Love books are published by
The Berkley Publishing Group
200 Madison Avenue, New York, NY 10016

To Claire Gerus-Ablitt,
editor, friend, and fellow healer...
who believed...

Chapter 1

"Is THIS THE best you can do?" Taylor Grant asked his partner dryly. With his shrewd police reporter's eye, honed for seven years in the trenches of New York City, he didn't miss a thing. Taylor's gaze narrowed critically on the menu he held in his large, lean hands.

"Hey, this is the best health-food restaurant in San Diego County, Taylor. Don't knock it." Barry settled comfortably into the well-padded booth as the restaurant began rapidly to fill to capacity with noontime patrons.

"I said I was hungry, not crazy. This is rabbit food. Isn't there *one* dish that has some meat in it?" Taylor scowled, his walnut-colored brows dipping with displeasure as he quickly perused the offerings on the menu.

"It'll do you good," Barry assured him. "You need vitamins, Taylor. At the moment, you look like hell—pasty-faced, circles under your eyes." He studied his friend for a moment and added, "Trust me: You're going to grow healthy and flourish here in the Land of Sunshine."

"The land of fruits and nuts, you mean," Grant said darkly. "And the only reason I don't have a tan is that I prowl around at night when the sun doesn't shine. It's not from poor health."

The photographer grinned broadly and gestured toward the crowded restaurant. "Do you see one unhealthy person in here?" he demanded. "Come on, raise your head and check it out!"

Grudgingly, Taylor lifted his square-jawed face to let his gray-eyed gaze sweep the room. "What I see is that most of these people look as though they could use a thick porterhouse steak. Put a little red blood into their gaunt-looking faces, Williams." Unhappily, he perused the menu, still hoping to find meat somewhere among the bizarre offerings.

"'Mung bean delight.'" Taylor groaned.

"Try the pita and alfalfa sprout sandwich," Barry suggested good-naturedly.

Taylor glared at him. "Do I look like a damn cow?"

"More like a bull ready to destroy a china shop."

"You're the one slinging around the bull about health food. I'm the one who's going to destroy you for talking me into coming here."

Barry, who was twenty-five, skinny and had a thatch of red hair, grinned happily. "Like I said, Taylor: You look terrible. After all, if I'm going to be photographer for a celebrated crime reporter, I have a vested interest in keeping him healthy. It only makes sense in terms of my career." Barry rubbed his long, large-knuckled hands together—like a man getting ready to eat a steak, Taylor mused gloomily.

He searched the menu a third time, trying to find a dish with a name he recognized. "There's a McDonald's across the street. I'll even settle for a fish sandwich, kid." In the next moment, Taylor chastised himself. He shouldn't call Barry Williams a kid. But hell, at thirty-five, he not only felt his age, he was tired. And it showed. He had gotten up grudgingly that morning and tripped over a box that had yet to be unpacked. Holding his injured big toe in his hands, he had hopped into the bathroom of his newly rented house. He hated anything bright in the morning. And that included the sun. He had no choice but to flip on the bathroom light, which destroyed what little good humor he had left.

The sight that met Taylor's blurred vision in the mirror wasn't exactly exciting. *Frightening* was a more accurate word. Dark shadows hovered beneath his bloodshot gray eyes, and his normally full, square face now seemed gaunt. First he had bumped his toe—it was still aching like crazy—and then he'd had to face himself. That hurt, too. He had tried to shave without making eye contact with his image in the mirror. Taylor's perverse sense of humor surfaced, and he added a new axiom to his growing list of sayings: Shaving with your eyes closed can be harmful to your face.

Raising his hand, he gingerly touched one of the razor cuts on his rock-hard jaw. Had that slash really been an accident, or had he been trying to slit his throat and get it all over with? Grant shook his head.

He reminded himself grimly that this was a fresh start. He had left his tension back east along with that frenzied job. This was California, and he had it made. No more investigative reporting of murders, rapes, and kidnappings. No more nightmares from which he would wake up to the sound of his own screams. He had a new job, an easier reporting load. No more of the tension that kept his gut twisted in a knot most of the time. For he was a victim of stress, the physician had informed him. And he was headed for an ulcer if he didn't make some changes in his life.

So he'd made a complete change, and he was beginning to regret it already.

"Taylor!" Barry hissed.

"What?"

"Where'd you disappear to? Man, you were a million miles away."

Don't I wish, Taylor thought unhappily. Maybe he should have taken a vacation between jobs. A long one. Maybe it hadn't been smart to leave one job, drive across country with his meager possessions, and begin working for the *Rio Conchos Sun* right away.

"Just a little tired," Taylor lied glibly, believing it was no one's business how he was really feeling. And then he winced slightly. Mary Ann had resented that attitude; she'd accused him of keeping himself closed up like a clamshell, never sharing his feelings with her. Savagely, he stuffed the dirty laundry of his memories away and forced himself to re-read the menu. "I'll try the grilled cheese sandwich. At least I know what's in it."

Barry relaxed his tall, skinny frame and grinned broadly. "It's served with a side order of tofu garnished with alfalfa sprouts."

"No french fries?"

"High in cholesterol, didn't you know?"

"Why don't these people let *me* worry about the state of my health instead of imposing their values on me?"

"Anybody drag you in here?"

"Yeah, you."

"I think you should get to know all the business people here in Rio Conchos. If any news breaks, they know to call our office. That way, we get it fresh and fast. Never hurts to make friends among the landed gentry, Taylor. And many of them come here to eat. This is an 'in' restaurant."

Taylor closed the menu as the waitress came over to take their order. Why did Barry have that look of glee on his youthful features? Was it his imagination or was Barry enjoying Taylor's discomfort? No, he reminded himself; he was just jaded and overly suspicious. But then the kid aimed a lopsided grin at him, his hazel eyes dancing, and Taylor's unease returned.

"Tomorrow I decide where we eat, Williams. Pay-back is a—"

There was a loud crash at the front of the restaurant. Out of instinct, Taylor Grant whirled around toward the noise. Everyone in the crowd had looked up momentarily, startled by the sound. Grant's gray eyes narrowed with intense concentration. A woman had entered through the brass-trimmed glass doors, a cumbersome load of books in her arms, and had apparently tripped. A dozen or so heavy volumes lay scattered helter-skelter at her feet. The distraught look on her perfectly oval face spurred Taylor into action. What was he doing? Sit back down, Grant. Ignoring his own order, he shot to his feet and strode toward the woman.

His reporter's eye quickly examined her face and clothing as he approached her, no detail escaping his thorough inspection. Black hair fell in a cloud around her proud shoulders and tumbled down over small, firm breasts hidden beneath a feminine peasant blouse. She looked like a Gypsy, he thought, slowing down as he approached her. The full skirt reminded him of a patchwork quilt: a burst of color against the stark whiteness of the simple blouse. Her flushed cheeks looked beautiful against the milky smoothness of her skin. Grant felt robbed of his breath as she tilted back her head and met his gaze. It was as if someone had struck him in the chest. He halted in front of her. The woman's eyes—a glorious blue, like polished lapis lazuli shot with molten gold in their vulnerable depths—met his startled gaze.

In the seconds that followed, it was almost as though lightning crackled between them. She looked young, her eyes wide open like a child's and filled with a deep trust of the world around her. Her lips, the color of a pomegranate, were parted, begging to be kissed—especially the full lower lip, which he suspected could form a teasing pout that would drive any male crazy. Groaning to himself, Grant tried to get control of his emotions. He *never* acted this way!

"Dumb!" Katie Riordan muttered, dropping to her knees, the patchwork skirt billowing around her in a profusion of color. She began to gather the books into a pile.

"Here, let me help you."

Her heart took a silly skip in her breast. Katie didn't know whether it was embarrassment over having caused a scene or the handsome stranger's piercing gray eyes as they touched her. "Thank you," she whispered breathlessly. "Oh, I feel so foolish!"

Taylor crouched down, picking up a few of the tomes, and smiled. She seemed as helpless as an autumn leaf twirling in a playful breeze. "Don't be embarrassed. It could happen to anyone," he soothed. And then he laughed at himself. What was he saying? When had he last reached out to make someone else feel at ease? Not for a long time . . . but then, she looked so much like a child that he couldn't help himself. Her black, curly hair shining with blue highlights tempted him to run his fingers through it; to stroke it into submission. He noticed her hands: beautiful, artistic hands, long and slender. There was a winsomeness about her; she was like a fragile princess appearing right out of the pages of a fairy tale. But it was her breathless freshness that made Taylor Grant feel an unfamiliar ache in the region of his heart. He envied her freedom of expression, that intangible quality that made her a blazing sunbeam in his darkened world.

She laughed. "Things like this happen to me all the time. Maud calls me Katie the klutz. And Claire, the owner of his restaurant, calls me Katie the whirlwind." Her mouth closed in silent amusement as she stretched her petite form to capture the last of the books. "I'm afraid I was in a hurry, as usual, a million things on my mind, when I came through those doors. I stubbed my toe . . ."

Taylor sat back on his haunches, watching her stack the books. "You and I have something in common, then. I stubbed my toe this morning, too."

She lifted her chin, unconsciously pushing that ebony mass away from one blazing cheek as she looked at him. "That's a sign that things are changing," she informed him. Her fluttering heart took another thump in her breast, and a magical warmth flowed through Katie as she met and drowned herself in his intelligent gray eyes, which reminded her of a hawk's. He had a face that some might shrink from: He wasn't handsome in the conventional sense. But to her he looked like a warrior. And then her imagination took flight. He was a knight, she decided, and he was tired from all the battles he had fought. She could see the exhaustion in those pewter depths. He seemed to look through her.

Katie found herself eagerly searching his face. He hid a great deal behind that implacable mask he wore. A square face, a strong jaw, a stubborn chin that dared anyone to try to change his mind. She laughed to herself. This man was self-sufficient—or tried to be—in every area of his life. She liked his broad shoulders and the controlled power that seemed to radiate from his body. Yes, she thought, he truly was a knight in shining armor. And if her intuition was working properly today—some days, she failed to listen to it and found herself in hot water!—this man was strong, with a heart-wrenching tenderness buried within his depths. But one look into those penetrating gray eyes and Katie knew he had not allowed anyone to get near his vulnerable, human side.

"Stubbing your toe means change?" he drawled.

"Absolutely. There's no such thing as an accident.

Everything happens for a reason."

A scowl gathered between his brows. Taylor lifted the books from the highly polished wood floor. Katie stood, a movement imbued with the grace of one who had studied ballet for years. She couldn't be over five-feet-two, he decided, even in her sandaled feet, but something about her carriage made her appear taller. Was it the tilt of her chin or the proud squaring of her small shoulders? "There's no reason for the way this world of ours works," he countered and placed the books in her waiting arms. His mind fled back to the horror of the crimes he had covered for seven grim years. "No reason," he muttered blackly.

Katie was stunned. She'd had no idea how tall he was until he stood. Not only were his shoulders broad, but his chest was massive above a narrow waist and hips. A cat, her imagination whispered. A wild, primitive animal lurked beneath the controlled surface of this man, in his short-sleeved burgundy shirt and charcoal-gray slacks. Taking a shaky breath, Katie forced a smile. "Thank you for helping me. That was very kind of you."

Taylor allowed his hands to rest languidly on his hips as he studied her. "Kind?" His voice sounded hard and jaded even to his ears. Why couldn't he be civil? Because he didn't *feel* civil. But she didn't deserve his caustic comments. No, there was a cleanliness and purity to her that was somehow slipping inside those walls he had erected around himself a long time ago. Taylor watched her face show distress at his gruff manner, and immediately he felt contrite. "Don't worry about it," he said stiffly, and turned away.

By the time Grant returned to his booth, she had seated herself at the last unoccupied table in the restaurant. He combed his fingers through his short, dark hair, angry with himself. You're a bastard, Grant. She just needed some help. You could have been a bit friendlier.

"Better hurry up and eat," Barry coaxed. "Your lunch will get cold."

Taylor picked up the sandwich and pried the slices of bread apart, warily eyeing the filling. Satisfied it was cheese with no unidentifiable additions, he moodily began to eat. Throughout the meal, Taylor kept one ear keyed to Barry's conversation and the other ear to the chatter surrounding them. But his gaze inevitably strayed back to the woman. What did she call herself? Katie the klutz? Katie the whirlwind? How could she sit quietly eating, yet seem to be in a constant state of animation? It was as if some energy radiated from her, like an invisible windstorm. Shaking his head, Taylor decided he was simply losing his mind. But then, he had never been normal. An abnormal childhood, an abnormal marriage, an exhausting job that had worn him out and made him cynical. Was it too late for him to change?

He rummaged around in his mind, trying to determine why Katie had affected him so profoundly. All he knew was that when his eyes fell into those lovely blue pools flecked with gold, he'd felt a stirring of hope. She was a romantic, he decided glumly, an idealist who tripped blissfully through life until somebody reached out to yank her back down into ugly reality. He was actually envious of her, he decided. But he hungered like a starving man for what she possessed, even though, simultaneously, he wanted to rip it from her. Life was harsh, after all, not some pie-in-the-sky fairy tale where dreams come true.

And every time Taylor lifted his head to stare moodily across the restaurant at Katie, he felt a longing that made him want to fling himself into her arms and feel her warmth around him. Be held and protected for just a moment. One moment . . .

His thoughts were short-circuited when a man five tables away suddenly clutched his chest and fell to the floor. Taylor was on his feet instantly. The other patrons froze, staring down at the man who lay gasping for breath.

Katie dropped her fork, horrified. Her large blue eyes widened as the stranger strode across the room like a jungle cat and dropped to his knees beside the victim. Her heart pounded as he leaned over the stricken man, who was thrashing wildly on the floor as if trying to get his breath. The stranger jerked the tie from the victim's throat and yanked open the collar and belt. The restaurant was heavy with shocked silence, and Katie realized the victim was having a heart attack.

"Does anyone here know CPR?" the rescuer thundered.

Katie blinked at the growling force of his voice. It was an in-charge voice that jarred the stonelike patrons. The victim's face was bluish-gray—he was nearly unconscious now—and she watched the stranger tilt the lolling head back.

"Move, dammit! I need help!"

Frustration warred with anger as Taylor glared up at Williams. The photographer shrugged apologetically. Figures, Taylor thought. What would a bunch of vegetarians know about real life?

Taylor keenly assessed the now unconscious man. Jerking his head up, he snarled, "Call an ambulance!"

As he was about to begin mouth-to-mouth resuscitation, Taylor saw a flash of color and watched the patchwork skirt settle opposite him. It was Katie, her eyes wide. For some reason, the closeness of her shook him. Before he could tell her what to do, she placed her left hand over the victim's heart. Taylor blinked once, aware of a mild tingling flowing up through his fingers, which were resting on the victim's neck and forehead. Suddenly, the man's bluish pallor was replaced by the flush of life. Color flowed back into his cheeks. What the hell was going on? Taylor started to speak, but Katie's hushed voice broke through his turmoil.

"Keep his head tilted back so he can breathe."

Taylor scowled darkly, keeping one hand on the man's neck to check his pulse. But his eyes were on Katie. He could feel something. But it wasn't visible. And it was unlike anything he had ever felt in his life. Katie was kneeling over the man, her slender white hand gently pressed to his chest, her expression rapt and—and what? Taylor wet his lips. Suddenly he was afraid. The man had been in the throes of a heart attack seconds before. As soon as Katie laid her hand on him, he had begun to recover.

Katie swallowed a lump in her throat, aware of the stranger's predatory gray eyes piercing her. The silence in the restaurant was ominous. Suddenly a camera flashed . . . once, twice, three times. Katie swung her head sharply away from Barry.

"No!" she cried, throwing out one hand. "Don't!"

Barry Williams ignored her, moving quickly around to Taylor to get a better shot. He clicked the camera twice more, ignoring Katie's protests. Excitedly he looked down at Taylor.

"Man, I don't believe this! Lucky we happened to be on the scene. I got some good pictures, Taylor. Man, this'll make a neat little feature story."

Oh, no! Katie bowed her head, anguish flooding her. This was the very thing she had sworn never to allow! She felt the eyes of the stranger examining her as if she were an insect under a microscope.

"Who are you?" Taylor rasped softly. "What are you—"

At that instant a team of paramedics burst into the restaurant, and Katie leaped to her feet. Quickly darting through the gathering crowd, she made it back to her table. Grabbing her purse, she whirled around, seeking escape. The restaurant's rear entrance was accessible, and she virtually flew down the hall and flung the back door open.

A strong hand closed firmly over her arm, bringing her to a halt just outside the door. Katie whirled, the cloud of black hair swirling around her pale face. She thrust out her other hand and met the hard, uncompromising wall of his chest. Her lips parted, and she gasped.

"You . . ." she whispered.

Taylor's eyes narrowed with keen intensity on her up-turned face. "I'm Taylor Grant, reporter for the *Rio Conchos Sun*. I want to know what just happened. Who the devil *are* you anyway? You put your hand on that man, and he immediately started to recover. The color came back to his face." He turned to look over his shoulder, toward the restaurant. "The paramedics say he's stable now." His gaze burned into her. "What did you do?"

Katie uttered a small whimper, trying to twist out of his grip. He wasn't hurting her, although he could have, with his long, strong-looking fingers wrapped around her upper arm. Her heart thrashed like a wild bird inside her breast. "Please," she begged, "let me go. Nothing happened. Nothing—"

"Something happened." His mouth curled into a blood-less smile. "I want your name and address. I need to find out more about you and—"

"No!" The cry was torn from her, and Katie wrenched out of his grip, stumbling backwards and almost falling. She pushed her hair from her eyes as she continued to breathe hard, her cheeks flushed scarlet. "Don't pursue this! Please don't! You don't understand. No one will."

Taylor shook his head determinedly. "Sorry, lady, I can't just back away. You're news, whether you want to be or not. You saved that guy's life!" And then mockery glinted in his eyes. "That is, unless you staged this whole thing for our benefit." His voice grew silken. "Sure you don't want some publicity? Did that guy put on an act?"

Katie's eyes flashed deep blue fire. "You are the most untrusting person I've ever met!" she sputtered indignantly. "I don't want anything from you, can you understand that? Just go away and leave me alone!" She wrenched her arm out of his grip and fled from him.

Taylor watched her run around the corner of the brick building and disappear. A slight smile hovered on his mouth. "Sorry, baby, I can't do that," he said softly. "You're either a very clever fake or a genuine miracle worker."

As he walked back into the restaurant, Taylor found himself hoping she really was a miracle worker. She was so incredibly beautiful . . .

"Man," Barry said with glee as he returned to their table, "that was eerie! I mean, she just kneeled down beside that guy and put her hand on him. And all of a sudden his color came back!" Barry shook his head wonderingly. "Who was she anyway?"

"That's exactly what I intend to find out," Taylor growled. He waited for the babble to die down after the paramedics had left with their stabilized patient. Then he strode up to the owner of the restaurant, introduced himself, and got her name.

Claire Garvey was shaken by the turn of events. Touching her brow, she frowned. "I'm sorry, who did you say you were?"

Taylor repeated his credentials, watching her face grow pale. "Who is that woman, Mrs. Garvey?"

"Why—uh, she comes in here to eat from time to time."

Taylor compressed his lips. "She mentioned you as if you were a friend, so you must know her last name. Where does she work?"

Claire's brown eyes narrowed suspiciously. "Why do you want to know, Mr. Grant?"

"Look," he said, his voice tinged with impatience, "this Katie might be a miracle worker, but it seems more than likely that she's a fake. Either way, it's a story, and I want to interview her. But I can't do that unless you'll tell me who she is." He grimaced: He was talking about Katie as if she were an object to be investigated, not a human being. It was obvious that Mrs. Garvey wasn't very happy with his attitude either.

"Now listen here," she said. "Katie is a very special person. Everyone loves her, and she is not a fake."

Taylor's eyes darkened. "You saw what happened."

"Yes, everyone did."

"And you're not surprised?"

Claire Garvey shook her head. "No, I'm not. As I said, Katie is special. Anyone she touches is better off for it."

Taylor had to concede the point. He had felt a strange sense of peace surrounding Katie as she knelt down beside the cardiac victim. And he had felt something else—a strange twinge in his heart—as he watched her rapt face. Katie had been in another world. How could he describe the glow on her face or the burning cobalt color of her eyes as she caressed the victim with her gaze? He mentally shook himself. Come on, Grant. Knock it off! You're getting soft. Soft-headed would be more like it. He focused his gaze on Claire Garvey, who appeared to be extremely nervous.

"Special in what way?"

"I can't discuss it with you, Mr. Grant. Katie's gifts are her own business, not mine."

Barry wandered over, tucking a roll of film into his pocket. "Hey, Taylor, I'm hoofin' it back to the darkroom. Gotta see how these shots turned out."

Claire frowned. "Really, Mr. Grant, you have no business writing anything about Katie or even taking her picture. She doesn't like publicity."

One eyebrow moved upward. "Oh?" Taylor said skeptically.

"Absolutely. Katie wants anonymity."

Taylor grinned. "She's not exactly going about it in the right way, is she, Mrs. Garvey?"

Claire Garvey glared up at him. "Leave her alone," she

said, enunciating every word.

Taylor lifted his chin, looking over at the table where Katie had sat. Her books were still piled there, in untidy stacks. That would help, he thought, a genuine smile tilting the corners of his mouth. "Thanks, Mrs. Garvey," he murmured, walking toward the table.

"I'll see you later, Taylor," Barry called.

"Right. I'll want to see those photos when I get back. Tell the editor I'll have the story ready for the evening edition." Taylor halted by Katie's table. Was it his imagination or could he smell the lingering lilac fragrance that seemed to surround her? He pulled a book from the stack and flipped through it, looking for a clue to her identity. There was a lavender sticker inside the back cover: Unicorn Bookstore. Picking up the whole stack of books, he went out the rear exit and walked to his black Trans Am.

Because he was still unfamiliar with Rio Conchos, which nestled against the wealthy area known as La Jolla, Taylor pulled out a street map. Committing the route to memory, he patiently refolded the map and placed it in the glove compartment. Perhaps someone at the Unicorn Bookstore would remember Katie, he mused, far more curious over the chain of events than he cared to admit.

Katie Riordan flew through the door of the Unicorn Bookstore. The silvery head of Maud Winthrop jerked up.

"Good grief, Katie, what on earth is the rush?"

Katie came to a halt, glancing around the store nervously. "Oh, nothing, Maud. Nothing. I'm sorry I'm late. Why don't you go along to lunch now?"

Maud came out from behind the desk that served as a cash register and office for the store. "Ain't been very busy since you left. Oh, Mrs. Clark called to say she's bringing Amanda to you. Seems the cat has a terrible cold and she was wonderin' if you'd help."

Distracted, Katie bumped into the corner of the dark

mahogany desk. "Ouch! Of course . . . uh, did you put her down with the other afternoon appointments, Maud?"

Maud, who was shaped like a plump pigeon, picked up her black leather purse. "Sure did, Katie. Have a nice lunch?"

Katie bit her lip. She never lied, but there was no sense in worrying Maud just because she herself was upset. "Let's put it this way: It wasn't boring. Now, shoo!"

Maud's brown eyes took on a lively twinkle. "Okay, okay. It takes me a minute to get my eighty-four-year-old body in gear. Do you need anything?"

Yes, Katie thought desperately. "No, thank you. Go on, I'll hold down the fort."

Maud walked out of the book store, and quiet settled in around Katie. Some of the strain disappeared from her face as she put on some music. Anything to soothe herself. She sat down and buried her face in her hands. The mass of black curls spilled around her shoulders. How could she have been so stupid? The man was a reporter! Oh, Lord, what was she going to do? And that photographer . . . Katie groaned, raising her eyes skyward.

"Okay, guys, I don't know what you're up to, but I don't like it," she muttered under her breath. "Not one bit." And yet, her eyes softened when she thought of Taylor Grant's strength, his masculinity, and that hidden streak of tenderness she had detected in him. And just as quickly, a flash of annoyance replaced her momentary peace. That cynic! How dare he intimate she was a fake! She rummaged through messy piles of bills and book orders on the desk. Well, if the cosmos was on her side, the whole incident would quickly blow over and be forgotten. Crossing her fingers for a moment, Katie closed her eyes and wished with all her might that the man named Grant would let the matter drop.

Chapter 2

TO KATIE'S DISMAY, the cosmos was not on her side. Barely half an hour had passed when the bell over the entrance tinkled, announcing a visitor. Looking up from the clutter on her desk, Katie felt her face go pale. Sunlight poured across the broad shoulders of Taylor Grant, surrounding him with a golden waterfall of light that illuminated his taut features.

He walked with the languid grace of that cat Katie had imagined earlier. Her heart skipped a few beats in panic as she felt his intense perusal. Willing herself to remain perfectly still, she thrust out her chin belligerently. Fearlessly she met his gray eyes.

"You forgot these," he said in silken tones, placing a stack of books—her books—on the only clear space on her desk.

"What? Oh, yes, thank you, Mr. Grant."

The silence grew as Katie watched him. Nervously, she crossed her arms, leaning back in the squeaky old office chair.

"Your friends are very protective of you, Katie."

She shivered at the huskiness of his voice as he used her name for the first time. Her lips parted at the smile in his thawing gray eyes. A warmth passed between them in the soothing seconds that followed. Grant's face lost some of its hardness, and she saw the exhaustion in it. But only for a split second. Then the unemotional mask was back.

"What do you mean, protective?"

"Mrs. Garvey wouldn't tell me your last name—or where you worked." He turned, taking in the clutter of the bookstore. It looked as if a cyclone had hit it. Stacks of books stood in miniature Towers of Pisa on the floor here and there, just begging to be shelved. Chaos reigned on every side. Huge Boston ferns hung from the low ceiling, their graceful green fronds arcing out in all directions. Several round tables were covered with blue-checked gingham cloths; tattered old chairs surrounded them. Bouquets of fresh white-petaled daisies and bright blue bachelor's buttons stood in the center of each table. The bookstore was rectangular in shape, with the desk near the door. Soft music issued from hidden speakers, soothing Taylor's taut nerves. In one corner stood a revolving rack, its compartments filled with dried herbs in plastic pouches. The books, he noticed with surprise, were randomly shelved; Katie apparently didn't believe in order—alphabetical or otherwise. He scowled. This place was in dire need of organization. Then Taylor looked back at Katie, realizing the Unicorn Bookstore mirrored her personality: It was exotic, endearing, old-fashioned, warm, and . . . He groped for another adjective to describe her.

"You own this place?" he asked brusquely, as he walked to a wall of shelves that held thousands of books.

"I do."

Taylor smiled slightly, hearing the defensiveness in her low voice. "How old are you, Katie . . . ?"

"Riordan, Mr. Grant. And I don't believe my age is of any concern to you."

He looked more closely at the books. Astrology, numerology, reincarnation, yoga, health food . . . He scowled darkly. Health food! Rabbit food, he thought tersely. But then, if Barry hadn't conned him into going to that restaurant, he'd never have met this enigma of a woman—or found the story. And she was worth it. "Katie Riordan. Nice Irish name."

"And I've got a temper to go with it, Mr. Grant. Now what do you want?"

Taylor lifted his finger, running it across the tops of several books. Dust. This place needed a good feather duster and at least a week's worth of loving attention. The purple carpeting was spotless, however, and Taylor saw no signs of poor housekeeping other than the dust and the general disorder. Her dark blue eyes clashed with his gray ones. "Is that a subtle threat, Katie Riordan?" he teased softly, his voice a cat's purr.

She licked her lips nervously. "No, of course not! I just want to be left alone, Mr. Grant, that's all. I want nothing to do with reporters."

"Then don't think of me as a reporter—just see me as a man."

She watched a smile tug at his sensual mouth and saw a new warmth flood his icy gaze. Groaning inwardly, Katie felt a blush rushing to her already hot cheeks. The nerve of the man! He was deliberately teasing her, her intuition warned. A cat playing with a helpless mouse. And she was dinner. Her cobalt eyes flashed indignation. "Save your teasing for someone else, Mr. Grant. I'm not interested."

"Are you married?"

"No, but—"

"Ah, you have a boyfriend."

She shot up off the old chair, which squeaked shrilly in protest. "I'm not a quarry to be pursued! Just tell me why you're here, and then leave!"

Taylor turned slowly to face her. In that blinding moment she took his breath away. She really did look like a Gypsy from the pages of a travel brochure, black hair swirling around her shoulders, the peasant outfit hiding her slight but very provocative figure, hands curled into small fists at her sides. His smile broadened. "Why don't you like reporters, Katie? Is it because you have something to hide?"

Her jaw went rigid, and her eyes flashed defiance. "Take your suspicions, Mr. Grant, and remove them—and yourself—from my store!"

Taylor wandered back to her. Carefully he monitored her expression. She had a fascinating face. It wasn't beautiful in the sense that a model's was, but it was unique. Each nuance of emotion flitted across her flushed features. He wondered what the texture of her flesh would be like and ached to reach out and brush a fiery cheek to find out. And those incredible eyes held mystery. He wanted to lean over and kiss each delicately framed lid, watch them open with desire. She was ethereal; that was the one word that described her. Would she disappear like mist on a hot summer's day? Flee like a frightened doe startled by a stalking hunter? Yes, she appeared defenseless . . .

"Tell me," he said. "Are you a fey spirit, or are you a fake?"

Katie blinked, and took a step away. "I'm not a fake. Don't take that accusing tone with me."

Taylor quickly masked his longing. This sorceress was indeed casting her spell on him. And she had done nothing but glare at him defiantly, with only a trace of fear in her wide, trusting eyes!

"There's no need to be afraid of me," he said, suddenly upset at the idea that she would fear him. He seldom lost his temper with a woman, though Mary Ann had goaded him often enough.

"I don't fear you, only what you'll put into print," Katie said, her voice suddenly weary. Her mouth lost some of its tension, and she chewed on her lip. "And you're going to write a story about me, aren't you, Mr. Grant?"

Why the hell did he feel guilty for doing his job? "Look," he said more roughly than he intended, "you did something to that man, and I want to know what it was." He paused. "Do you really own this bookstore?" he asked, wanting to change the subject.

"Yes," she answered, all her defiance dissolving.

Taylor cursed himself; she was making him feel like a first-class heel.

"What are all these odd volumes? They're not the usual thing you find in bookstores."

Katie sat down in the chair, rubbing her temple where a headache was threatening to begin. "Would you be less suspicious if they were pornographic? I suppose so. You're used to dealing with the misery of life—not its joy."

Taylor gave her a guarded look. "How do *you* know what I'm used to?"

She shrugged tiredly. "You've spent a lot of time investigating crimes. I can feel it around you." And then she lifted her head, meeting his incredulous gaze. "Or is the truth too unsettling? I should lie and say I read it somewhere; then you would have believed me."

There was a lingering sadness in her tone. And she had hit on the truth, Taylor admitted grudgingly. He suddenly wanted to ask her a hundred more questions, but saw the fatigue in her eyes. Again he felt a twinge of guilt. "Do you always tell the truth?"

"Even if it hurts," she said ruefully, a slight smile on her lips. But it was that same sad smile that tore at his carefully protected heart—and made him feel guilty.

"What did you do to that man?"

"I touched him."

"Well, so did I, and he sure as hell didn't stop gasping and choking when I did it."

"You called for help. I came because you asked me to. Once someone has made a request of me, I'm bound by cosmic law to help. It's as simple as that."

He stared. "Lady, there's *nothing* simple about you."

Katie managed a patient smile. "Oh, I'm very simple, Mr. Grant. Transparent, so I'm told."

"Then why are you evading my question?"

"I thought I answered it."

"Then maybe I didn't ask it clearly."

Katie inclined her head. "You're an intelligent man, Mr. Grant. I was hoping your heart would be in the right place, too."

He bridled at her words. "I don't get paid to listen to my heart, Miss Riordan. Every time I allowed myself to get involved with the people I was investigating, I paid a huge emotional price. That's unacceptable to me. So we'll just leave my feelings out of this and get on with the reason I'm here."

She flinched at the anger in his voice. It wasn't out of fear, however. Katie felt his pain, and she closed her eyes, massaging her temples. She was annoying him, but she had to be discreet—something it was terribly hard for her to be.

"Very well, Mr. Grant." Katie opened her eyes and focused on his pale countenance. The anger and pain she saw in his gray eyes made her want to cry for him. He must have gone through a private hell, to be reacting this way. Getting up, she placed a teakettle on a hot plate. "Would you like some herb tea? I'm going to have some."

Taylor shook his head, angry that she'd been able to intuit so much about him when after all, they were strangers. Katie unsettled him, unstrung him, left him off-balance and wanting . . . Lord, wanting simply to grip her in his arms and hold her. Hold her, feel that warm, feminine body against his. Her warmth against the frigid cold inside him. She could thaw him, make him feel again, he realized.

"I've got a deadline to meet," he said, forcing his mind to return to the subject at hand. "Now, either you tell me what you did or I'll print this article without your help."

Katie reached for a mug with a brightly painted rainbow on it and selected a tea bag from a box. "I'll answer your questions," she said quietly.

"Are you a witch?"

Katie gasped, whirling toward him. "A witch!" Her blue eyes grew furious. "Where did you get that idea?"

"Well, all these books on astrology—"

"Astrology is *not* witchcraft, Mr. Grant. Before you jump to conclusions, why don't you look at the shelves? You'll find nothing on witchcraft here—and you never will. Not so long as *I'm* the owner."

"Then what kind of bookstore is this?"

"A metaphysical bookstore, that's what!"

Taylor glared darkly at her. "Want to give me your definition of metaphysics, Miss Riordan?"

The teakettle whistled shrilly, and Katie pulled it from the hot plate. Her hand trembled as she poured hot water into the cup; some splashed out onto the small counter. Muttering under her breath, Katie banged the teakettle back down and stooped to retrieve some paper towels. "*Meta*, Mr. Grant, means 'beyond.' And if you add *physics* you have 'beyond physics.'" Her blue eyes were flashing dangerously, but she kept her voice down. "It is the study of the unseen, that which we cannot weigh or measure with our present technology, but which surely exists—just as you and I do."

He noticed that when she was angry, the color rushed into her cheeks and a display of fireworks flashed in her deep blue gaze. The ebony sheen of that glorious black mane made Taylor long to run his fingers through it. "Give me an example of metaphysics at work."

She turned her back on him, drowning the tea bag viciously in the hot water. "You saw it in action today, Mr. Grant. Now leave," she hissed. "Because you and I have no common ground on which to understand each other. You clearly know nothing of these topics. And I won't tolerate your obvious contempt when you won't make the slightest effort to understand the world I live in."

He combed his fingers through his hair, trying to understand her. "You're right: I don't believe in any of that junk, seen or unseen. What counts, lady, is the real and very ugly world right outside that door." He punched a finger in the direction of the street. "Hell, you could get robbed right here in the store."

Katie faced him, the mug of tea cradled between her long, expressive fingers. The anger had vanished; her eyes now held a mixture of sadness and understanding. "That won't happen."

"Oh?"

"Don't ask for an explanation, Mr. Grant. You'd probably roll on the floor and die of laughter. Suffice it to say I've been running this bookstore for five years and I've encountered no criminals."

Grant planted his hands on his hips, drawn to her despite himself. "If you don't give me a clear and specific explanation of what you did to that cardiac victim, Miss Riordan, I'm going to write the article from my perspective only."

Katie tried to still her pounding heart. "You'll write it the way *you* see it no matter what I say, Mr. Grant. Any explanation I gave you would be superfluous." After a quiet moment during which she seemed to reconsider the situation, she threw him a pleading look. "Please don't write the story. It's not as significant as you make it out to be. The only important thing is that the man will live."

"How do you know he will?"

"I know," she answered stubbornly. "Why don't you check with the hospital?"

"Oh, I intend to do just that, Ms. Riordan, as soon as I get some straight answers out of you."

Her blue eyes rounded. "I've given you answers!" she said, her temper flaring.

"Politician's answers. Answers that tell me nothing." He admired her spunk, her strength of spirit, despite the differences between them. "Well, I'm not known for printing evasions. I haven't made a name for myself doing that."

She sat down, glaring up at him. "Mr. Grant, you made up your mind hours ago about what happened in that restaurant. Nothing I could say would change your cynical opinions."

A brief grin creased the corners of Taylor's mouth. "Oh, yes it would." He wanted to know more about her. She was interesting—and utterly different from any woman he had met. The face of a child and the body of a woman, he thought. And a guileless quality that beckoned like a light in the darkness of his heart. And then he reminded himself that women were rarely helpless. Or vulnerable. They only appeared that way. Her fine, thin brows knit with vexation at his persistence.

"If you think for a moment that you threaten me or—"

Taylor laughed deeply. It was the first time in ages. "I like your honesty, Ms. Riordan. And if we didn't have this little matter of a newspaper story standing between us, I would like to know you better." He recoiled within himself. What was he saying? Hadn't he extricated himself from his marriage only one short year ago? His life was better *without* serious commitment to a woman. So why did he want to get to know her? Annoyed with himself, Taylor shook his head.

Katie clamped her lips shut, coloring hotly in the wake

of his compliment and frank expression of interest. She felt drawn to him, whether she wanted to be or not. "I told you, we have nothing in common. Whether or not you print that story."

Taylor shrugged. "Too bad. Well, I'm leaving now. That article and photo will appear in this evening's *Sun,* Ms. Riordan. I strongly suggest you call me if you have anything to add." He placed his business card in front of her. Again, Taylor felt a twinge of guilt as she looked up at him, her eyes filled with a fear he didn't understand.

"You do what you must, Mr. Grant," she whispered faintly.

"Well," Barry said, sauntering up to Taylor's desk, "what did you find on out about our Gypsy lady?" He placed four photos in front of him, each showing Katie leaning over the cardiac victim.

Taylor scowled and stopped typing as he scooped up the pictures. Dammit, he shouldn't feel guilty! Katie wore an ethereal expression, kneeling by Joe Collins, the heart attack victim.

"*Gypsy* is a good word," Taylor muttered as he checked each photo. Katie looked very feminine, the glossy mane of hair framing her delicate features. "I made some phone calls, Barry. Among other things, I learned that the chief of police has gotten some complaints about her."

Barry sat down on the edge of the desk, making himself comfortable. "Oh?"

"Yeah. From time to time her bookstore features speakers on astrology, numerology, et cetera. Apparently some of the townspeople don't believe in that nonsense, and three of them have lodged complaints against her." Taylor smiled distantly. "She has no police record, though. The complaints appear to come from a few people who enjoy stirring up the dust."

"Were you able to track the complainants down?

"All three of them." He pointed to the notes he had taken as he talked to the complainants. "It amounts to a clash between their beliefs and Katie's." Why had he used her first name in such a personal way? She was just another story. A subject to be studied, investigated at arm's length, and nothing more.

"Katie's right to freedom of speech is getting trampled by her enemies?" Barry inquired, grinning.

"That's all."

"So what did they have to say about her?"

Taylor rubbed his jaw, leaning back in the chair, his gray eyes dark with intensity. "One called her a witch. Another said she was a menace to society and ought to be locked away. The third called her a fake."

Barry's red eyebrows moved upward. "Fake? Did the caller go into detail?"

Taylor smiled lazily. "Apparently our Katie Riordan is a healer. You know, laying on of hands and all that? The third complainant called her a quack and a fake. Said she didn't really heal the animals over at the veterinary hospital, like everyone said she did."

"Jeez, this is getting interesting. Why didn't I know about this before?"

Taylor sat up. "Good question. Maybe that's why the boss fired my predecessor. Any idiot knows enough to make a daily check of the police records to find out what complaints were lodged. It didn't take much to find out all about Katie."

"I've lived in Rio Conchos for three years and never heard her name mentioned," Barry said disbelievingly. "And in light of her performance at the restaurant, I think that's a crime. She really is fodder for a good feature story."

"I think so, too. I just got off the phone with the Collins family's physician. And you know what he told me?"

"What?"

"That heart attack Collins suffered in the restaurant should have killed him on the spot." Grant scowled. Collins is in surgery right now. I'll know more about his condition after he gets out."

"That's pretty sobering when you stop to think about it," Barry agreed. "So the doctor's saying Collins should have died right there on the spot and he didn't?"

"You got it." Taylor's mouth moved into a thin line. "He's alive right now because of Katie."

"She tell you anything?"

"No. Closed up like a clam. I tried to call the restaurant owner again, but she refused to come to the phone. I've nothing but the negative reports on Katie. No one who might say anything positive about her wants to talk."

"That's too bad."

"Yeah," Taylor groused, as he returned to typing the article. "I'll have this piece finished in a few minutes. I like the photos you took. Let's use number three," he said.

Unhappily Barry stood and picked up the photo. "Too bad we don't have the time to investigate this in depth. I have a feeling a whole lot is being left unsaid. How about the vet hospital? Any luck?"

"Nope. The vet's out on an emergency call at a horse farm and the secretary 'doesn't know a thing.'"

"Great, just great."

Yeah, Taylor thought with disgust, just great. He was baffled by Katie's behavior. Why hadn't she defended herself? It appeared that publicity wasn't her motive after all. Three complaints had already been lodged against her, and she'd made no attempt to pump them up into headlines. One corner of his mouth twitched in annoyance. He found himself wanting to protect her, dammit. From herself, if necessary. Once this story came out, the people who disapproved of Katie Riordan would have new ammunition. But she had already won the first battle—by saving a man's life. And his reportage of that fact would cause still more gossip, making life even harder for her. And he would be responsible. Taylor cursed himself for believing that moving to a smaller city would make news reporting any less painful. Hammering mercilessly on the typewriter, out of frustration and disgust, he rapped out the last couple of sentences and finished the article.

Chapter 3

TAYLOR HAD BARELY reached his desk the next morning, a cup of coffee in hand, when the phone began to ring. In the first hour, there were ten calls from residents of Rio Conchos—about Katie Riordan. Editor-in-chief Dean Gerus emerged, beaming, from his office just as Taylor was hanging up after the final call.

"We're in the money, Taylor. Several West Coast dailies are going to carry your story along with the photo." He rubbed his hands together with unabashed enthusiasm, his face wreathed in a smile. "This is great. I hire you, and inside of a week, our newspaper gets a name." He slapped Taylor on the back. "Hell of a story. You did a good job."

Taylor frowned, finishing off his cold coffee. He got up to pour another cup from the dented percolator in the corner. Syndication of his story meant a nice chunk of money for the newspaper, and Taylor's byline in several area papers. But he felt no elation as he wondered what the notoriety would do to Katie Riordan, who had tried so hard to safeguard her privacy. He stood near the coffee shelf, pondering the whole sordid mess. He hadn't slept well last night; his thoughts—and, whether he wanted to admit it or not, his heart—were centered on Katie. Those huge lapis lazuli eyes were meltingly warm; life danced in their dark depths. He wondered what it would be like to hear Katie laugh. Well, chances were he wouldn't get that opportunity now.

The door to the small, cramped newspaper office flew open, hitting the wall with a loud thwack and getting everyone's undivided attention. Taylor raised his head and turned toward the noise. Katie Riordan, a copy of the *Rio Conchos Sun* in her hand, burst through the door like a tornado. Taylor's breath caught in his chest as he drank in her fiery beauty. The mass of raven-colored hair was caught up in a red ribbon so that it didn't hide the beauty of her flushed face. Today she was dressed in the style of the late eighteen hundreds. The off-white muslin dress did everything for her petite figure, the lace at her throat and cuffs accenting her haunting femininity. And those eyes . . . Taylor shook his head as if to cast off her magical spell. But just as soon as Katie's narrowed gaze caught and locked with his, she turned from a Victorian maiden into a wild-eyed tigress.

"You!" she cried, swinging the paper angrily over her head as she approached him. "You—you miserable excuse for a human being!" She halted inches from him, waving the newspaper under his nose. "How dare you!" she sputtered, her voice strained and quavering. "How could you write such garbage?"

"Calm down, Miss Riordan," Taylor growled.

"Calm down! How would you feel if some idiot reporter wrote such lies about *you?* I'm not a sorceress. Or a fake, as you've reported!"

Taylor's mouth drew into a grim line. "Look, I asked for your side of it, but you refused to discuss the incident. What do you expect?"

Katie uttered a very unladylike expletive. For the first time in her life she wanted to strike someone. Grant's maddening calm only added fuel to the fires of rage. "I told you my side of it!"

"Well, you didn't elaborate sufficiently, shall we say?"

Tears filled her eyes, making them seem even more luminous. Angrily, she dashed them away. She wouldn't cry in front of this creep. "You're the most insensitive boor I've ever had the misfortune to meet! Do you have any idea what kind of phone calls I've been getting?" She raised the paper over her head. "Crank calls! Threatening calls!" She drew herself up, anguish mirrored in her haunted expression. "I've tried never to hurt anyone or anything, Mr. Grant. I haven't always succeeded, but I've always tried to do what was right. Joe Collins is alive today, isn't he? But instead of reporting on *that* side of it, the positive side, you print *this* outrageous nonsense. Just to sell newspapers, to win another journalism award. Well, you may be a big-time reporter with a national reputation, but you've lost your humanity somewhere along the way!" She threw the paper down at his feet. "I hope you feel horrible about this. But I doubt if you have even one shred of remorse. I doubt you're able to feel *anything!* Welcome to Rio Conchos, Mr. Grant. I hope you enjoy your stay here while you go about destroying people's lives!"

Grimly, he set his coffee down, his anger at war with his guilt. Before he could say a word, Katie had whirled from the office, the door swinging widely in the wake of her exit. Cursing, he followed her out and saw her heading toward the small parking lot. He caught up with her just as she reached a beat-up black Volkswagen Beetle.

"Katie—wait, dammit!" He grabbed her arm and gently pulled her to a stop.

"Let me go!" she cried, jerking out of his grasp.

Taylor's heart wrenched in his chest as he saw the tears rolling down her flushed cheeks. "Look," he began haltingly, "I didn't mean—"

"Oh, yes you did! Big-time reporter moves to a small town to make a name for himself at other people's expense. Well, you've done it, Mr. Grant. Now live with it while I try to deal with all the crank calls!"

"I didn't mean to hurt you. But dammit, you left me no alternative when you wouldn't cooperate!"

She flattened herself against the Volkswagen as he came within inches of her. Her heart was pounding furiously in her breast, but in spite of her rage, she was wildly aware of him as a man. She saw the anguish in his gray eyes as he groped for words to appease her. Angrily, she brushed the tears from her cheeks. "Cooperate? Aren't I entitled to my privacy? What remains of it," she added bitterly.

He gave her a wary look. "I've received ten phone calls in the past hour. About half have been in support of you," he admitted, his voice strained. "For your information, I tried to interview people who knew you, Miss Riordan; but they all refused to comment."

Her eyes narrowed dangerously. "As well they should. My private life belongs to me—not to you and not to that damn newspaper you sell your soul to for a living."

Grant felt his anger stirring. "Let me tell you something, lady. I've learned what life is like in the dank streets of some of New York's toughest neighborhoods. Your flaky attitude wouldn't allow you to survive in the real world for five minutes! So don't judge me, and don't criticize my ethics."

Her nostrils flared and she pursed her full lips. "I don't judge anyone. Your actions speak for themselves!"

"The blame for this article rests on your shoulders, not mine," he said ominously.

She was trembling visibly. "I don't want to argue any

further," she said, backing down a little. "I'd just like to know what to do about these anonymous phone calls, Mr. Grant. I've lived here for five years and gotten along fairly well with everyone. Now I have one caller threatening to set fire to my bookstore and another threatening to throw a Molotov cocktail through the window. Thanks to you."

Taylor's anger faded as the cold reality of what she was saying hit him. There was no way he wanted to see her hurt. She was too special—and too naive. And something about her brought out the protectiveness in him. Cursing softly, Taylor held up both hands in a gesture of peace.

"Look, I'm sorry about the calls. I certainly didn't want that to happen." The look she gave him said she didn't believe him, but he went on anyway. "Let me talk to the police. We'll get your phone tapped so that any future calls can be traced."

Stubbornly she crossed her arms, her eyes blazing with deep blue fire. "I'm surprised you would offer. If someone bombed my bookstore, that would make the front page, too—probably under your byline! And isn't that what you're really after? No, thanks, I'll take care of this in my own way. You've done enough damage." Her features were still taut with anger. "It's your job to destroy people, isn't it?"

Taylor reared back as if he had been struck. Dumb-founded, he watched her slide into the Volkswagen and drive off. Mary Ann had said almost the same thing: *Do you always destroy everything?* Anguished, he bowed his head, trying to think clearly amid the seething emotions Katie had unleashed.

"Damn you, Taylor!" Mary Ann had screamed. "You've destroyed our marriage! You've turned your life upside down for your damn career! And now look at you," she sobbed, "you're ready to break. Why couldn't you have compromised? Why did you have to destroy everything? *Why?*"

Taylor took in a deep, steadying breath, vaguely aware that he had been gasping. Slowly he walked back to the newsroom. It had been a year since the divorce. A year of living alone and burying himself deeper in his job. His gray eyes darkened with pain as he admitted to himself that he had indeed destroyed his marriage. What was it within him that drove him over the brink time after time? Why couldn't he ever be moderate in his actions? And now, he had done it all over again. But the outcome was the same: Somebody had ended up irrevocably wounded. In this case, Katie Riordan. Guilt surged through Taylor. Damn his journalistic standards. Why couldn't he have tempered the article? He had, as usual, gone for the jugular. And who was bleeding because of his uncompromising stance? Katie. Sweet, harmless Katie whose honesty was a breath of fresh air to his darkened soul.

Miserably, Katie set the phone in its cradle—for what seemed like the hundredth time that day. Maud put a cup of herb tea in front of her and gave her a motherly pat on the shoulder.

"Come on, Katie, drink up. It's chamomile. Good for the nerves. Let me take the next few calls. You just go upstairs to your apartment and call it a day," she soothed.

Katie took the mug and sipped at its golden contents. "I'll be okay, Maud. Really, I will. It's just so upsetting. All these horrible calls."

Maud's brown eyes narrowed ferociously. "Well, if that Grant fella hadn't painted you as some sort of-of—"

"'Sorceress,'" she muttered grimly. "I suppose I should be grateful that he didn't say 'witch.'"

"Humph! Might as well have, for all these silly calls! Witch, indeed! Since when is healing and helping sick animals and people a sin *or* a crime! What's this world coming to?" Maud moved slowly from behind the desk to pick up a stack of books that needed to be shelved.

Katie's blue eyes grew warm as she watched Maud. What would she do without her? When both her parents had died in an airplane crash, a large part of Katie died with them. And yet, the cosmos, in all its infinite wisdom, had provided Maud as her new mother only days after their death. Warmth flowed through Katie, and she closed her eyes momentarily, dwelling on the love Maud gave so freely to everyone. She glanced at her watch: it was only noon. Katie wished it was closing time . . .

"Look at this," Maud exclaimed. She shut the door to the bookstore and held out a copy of one of the largest newspapers on the West Coast.

Despair washed over Katie as she saw her photograph on page three, along with Taylor Grant's story. Groaning, she shut her eyes.

Maud watched her worriedly. "Does that mean more phone calls than what we've been receiving already?"

"I'm afraid so," Katie said, tossing the paper on the desk. It was eight o'clock, time to close the bookstore. The last of the curiosity seekers had left. She turned, rummaging through several drawers to find the key. "Why don't you go home, Maud? It's been a very long day."

"And a busy one. I guess all that publicity wasn't entirely negative. We've had record sales today. That should help with the mortgage payment you were so worried about."

"Always a silver lining, right?" she mused, getting up to give Maud a quick hug. "Go on home, Maudie. You've put in too many hours today, and you're looking tired."

"Humph! At eighty-four I can still work a twelve-hour day without flagging." She waggled her finger in Katie's grim face. "You close this store up right now. And then you get yourself a nice hot bath and just relax. And no stayin' late to balance the books."

Katie smiled as she walked Maud to the front door. "Yes

ma'am. I'll see you at noon tomorrow. Good night."

Maud's round face drew into a beatific smile as Katie leaned over and gave her a peck on the cheek. "Good night," she said.

The April evening was turning cooler, and Katie decided to leave the door open and welcome the fragrant smell of spring flowers. Her brow wrinkled in a worried frown as she approached the desk and picked up the accounting book and the box of unpaid bills. The fresh country air was far preferable to the lifeless chill of air conditioning. And right now she'd rather be taking a long walk in the hills that surrounded the quaint town, simply allowing nature to lift her depression.

"Why the hell did you leave the door open? Didn't you say you've been receiving threatening calls?"

Katie whirled around, the cigar box flying out of her hands and scattering the mass of unpaid bills on the floor at her feet. Taylor Grant's huge figure blocked out the overhead light and brought a startled cry from her lips. Her heart pounded wildly at the base of her throat, and automatically her hand went to her breast.

"You scared me to death!"

Grant's scowl deepened. "You have no business leaving a door unlocked when it's dark outside—let alone wide open."

She took several deep breaths. And then, to her annoyance, registered all the bills on the floor. Dropping to her knees, she began to collect them. Grant crouched, too, and helped her with the task.

"What do you want? Haven't you done enough damage in one day, Mr. Grant?"

"I came to talk to you."

Her heart thumped in response to the velvet tones of his voice. Katie looked up from her position on her hands and knees and stared directly into his face, only a few feet away. Her anger dissolved as she perceived the exhaustion in his gray eyes. Wetting her lips, she sat back, slender hands resting on her thighs. "I suppose I owe you an apology, too." She gestured gracefully. "In fact, I tried to call you. I said something I shouldn't have—and I'm sorry, Mr. Grant. But the sheer volume of people calling and visiting the Unicorn has been overwhelming. I couldn't get away." She smiled. "I couldn't even get an outside line on the phone."

Grant grunted, eyeing the bills as he continued to collect them. "I tried to call you a couple times, too."

Her expression softened. "You did?"

Taylor looked into her puzzled face. How had she grown more lovely in twelve hours' time? he wondered. When he saw the shadows of fatigue skirting her lovely blue eyes, he experienced a twinge of conscience. "Yeah. I wanted to confess. A syndicate picked up the story and now it's being printed in every major newspaper on the West Coast."

"Don't be so glum. It's not going to hurt your career."

He studied a couple of the bills and then handed them to her. Their fingers met briefly, and he was conscious of the warmth and softness of her hand. He wondered if the rest of her was as warm and responsive, quickly realizing that she was. "That's no longer important to me. You are."

A thrill raced through Katie's heart at these words. She pulled over the battered old cigar box, dropped the bills into it unceremoniously, and forced the frayed lid closed. There was an undeniable magnetism about this man, and suddenly Katie had the wild urge to reach out, throw her arms around his neck, and bury herself against that massive chest. There was a protectiveness about him, it radiated toward her. He's probably feeling guilty, she thought, trying to dismiss the heated awareness of her body.

"I don't understand."

Taylor managed a smile and rested his arms on his well-muscled thighs. "Something told me to talk to you once more before I released that story, but I didn't do it."

"You didn't listen to your intuition."

"No, I didn't." He sighed heavily. As he stood, Taylor offered her his hand.

Katie lifted her chin. Her lips parted as she stared up at him. He was so tall and masculine! Without even thinking, she placed her hand in his and watched as it was swallowed up. Taylor pulled her to her feet and reluctantly released her hand. Momentarily dizzy, she took a few steps backward and bumped into the desk.

"You had dinner yet?" he asked.

Katie shook her head. "No, I usually make something in my apartment after I close the bookstore."

"Let me buy you dinner. It's the least I can do."

Katie's heart wrenched as she heard the fatigue in his deep, mellow voice and saw it in the planes of his face. There was something boyishly vulnerable about him in those fleeting seconds, and Katie responded to what she felt. "All right," she murmured, setting the bill box back on the desk.

Taylor managed another smile. "Thanks."

She retrieved her shoulder bag and walked toward the entrance. Taylor followed her, halting as she began to search through the purse.

"I think you left the keys on the desk."

"Oh? Oh, yes. Dumb of me!" She whirled to retrieve the keys. Smiling, she joined him outside. "I do this all the time. Maud swears she's going to put a ball and chain on my leg to slow me down, so that I don't get ahead of myself."

Taylor tested the locked door. Satisfied, he slipped his hand beneath her elbow and led Katie around the brick building to the parking lot in back. "A ball and chain?" he murmured dryly. "Somehow I don't think that would work. How can you stop a butterfly from flitting about?" He gazed down at her, aware of the blue highlights in her hair, brought out in the soft light of sulfur lamps that stood like sentinels in the parking lot.

Katie felt heat rush into her cheeks. So there *was* some sensitivity to him after all! "I've been called a scatterbrain, terminally forgetful, and several other less flattering things, but never a butterfly."

"You're a butterfly, Katie Riordan," Taylor assured her, opening the door of the Trans Am for her. "You're a willful free spirit in a day and age that doesn't encourage such individuality. And that," he said, his voice a low growl, "is what has gotten you into trouble."

Katie snapped the seat belt across her lap and waited for him to get in the car. "What are you talking about, Mr. Grant?"

"Call me Taylor." The shadows played across his strong features as he turned to look at her. "I've thought a lot about you today," he began, "and I've come to the conclusion that you're one of those special people who exist for themselves, regardless of what society may think." His gray eyes grew tender. "And I just clipped your wings—by putting that article to press. I should have come back and gotten your side of the story."

The tension between them increased. Katie held her breath as he reached over, lightly brushing her flushed cheek. It was as if he were stroking a priceless gift, and a string of explosions occurred along her nerve endings, sending pleasure coursing through her body.

"You don't clip a butterfly's wings," he muttered, his brows dipping. "They're too fragile."

Her eyes grew merry with mischief. "I'm hardly fragile, Mr.—I mean, Taylor. Just because I'm only five feet two doesn't mean I can't stand up on my own."

His laughter rumbled as he turned the key. The Trans Am purred to life like a huge, contented cat. "I know that, Katie. Remember: I was on the receiving end of your anger." He drove out of the lot and made a right turn onto the main street of Rio Conchos.

"I wasn't angry, Taylor. I was upset by the injustice of that story. You didn't give me a fair shake."

He nodded, pursing his lips. "You're right. And for some reason, I want to atone for my mistake."

"Just having you admit it makes me feel better," Katie said. "You don't have to buy me dinner, too."

His smile reminded her of a cat who had cornered its next meal. "This is the first time in my reporting career that I've allowed myself the luxury of admitting I made a mistake. Before, I would just rationalize it away and shrug it off." His gray eyes held that same tender spark as he glanced over at her rapt features. "But a certain fey Irish princess brought this tendency to my attention, and I decided it was time to examine myself with the same ruthless objectivity I used to limit to the practice of my profession."

Katie shivered. "Everyone's allowed to make mistakes, Taylor. That's how we all learn. I know you didn't print that story to deliberately hurt me. I don't sense that you're cruel by nature."

His mouth drew tight. "I've been accused of being very ruthless, Katie. And I've heard it from all corners, so don't be so quick to let me off the hook."

She folded her hands in her lap and gave a shake of her head. "You're opinionated, stubborn, and single-minded. But you're not deliberately cruel," she repeated doggedly.

He gave her a wry smile. "Do you always go to bat for the poor, maimed, and unfortunate, Katie Riordan?"

Her answering smile tore at his senses. "I believe that each human being is special and individual, Taylor. I try not to categorize people, but to treat each as a unique entity."

Parking the Trans Am, he shook his head. "How do you manage to stay alive in this world with views like that?"

Laughing, Katie shrugged. "I don't know. What's wrong with treating each person as a rare and beautiful flower unfolding in your presence?"

Drawn to her clear, effortless laughter, Taylor reached over, his eyes suddenly hooded and probing. "You're wrong," he said thickly, caressing her cheek, "you're the rare flower, Katie. So delicate, so fragile . . . I find myself wanting to protect you from this ugly world we live in. I'm afraid that someday soon your pristine spirit will be crushed by reality . . ."

Black lashes fanned out across her cheeks, and she trembled beneath his touch. Despite his powerfully masculine aura, his touch was gentle, making coals of yearning brightly burn to life, deep within her responsive body. Opening her eyes, Katie offered him a tender, tremulous smile. "I'll be all right, Taylor. I've managed to survive for twenty-six years. Life's been good to me." She shrugged. "Or maybe I've been good to life and I'm merely reaping the benefits . . ."

Taylor wanted to continue his exploration of the jade-smooth skin beneath his hand. He wanted to follow that stubborn jawline down to her slender neck and plant small kisses on her throat. He wanted to feel Katie respond to him. He noticed the hardening of her nipples through the soft muslin of her dress as he caressed her cheek. And her eyes were wide and languorous, telling him just how much he was affecting her. Her response made Taylor feel good about himself, and he hadn't felt that way in a long time. Reluctantly, he withdrew his hand from her face. She was indeed a butterfly: fragile, beautiful, and free.

"Come on, I owe you a dinner," he said more gruffly than he intended, as he slid out of the car. Katie's world was fantasy. Nothing more. His world was the real one, the one where pain, suffering, and harshness resided, day in and day out. But still he longed to be part of her magical environment, if only for a few hours. Taylor felt as if he were coming out a long, dark tunnel through which Katie represented the light of day . . .

Chapter 4

"YOU DIDN'T HAVE to take me to the most expensive restaurant in town," Katie protested, as she opened the menu.

"Why not? You're worth it."

She eyed the menu speculatively, trying to ignore the overtures her body was making toward Taylor Grant. He took her breath away, simply by daring to be honest—and thereby, vulnerable. Peeking at him over the edge of the menu, Katie wondered what it had cost him to admit he was wrong in publishing the article without getting her side of the story.

"Tell me about yourself," she urged, setting the menu aside and folding her hands beneath her chin.

A smile tugged his sensual mouth. "Isn't that my line?"

"Why should it be? I asked because I'm interested."

"I'm not used to baring my soul."

Her blue eyes sparkled with mischief again. "When were you born?"

Taylor gauged her in the silence, enjoying her inquisitiveness. Her black hair curled behind the bright red ribbon, emphasizing the clean lines and planes of her face. "Now, why would you want to know that?"

She laughed, clapping her hands delightedly. "You're so wary! You must be a Scorpio. They're always so secretive."

He shrugged his broad shoulders, the tension flowing from his body. This was what he needed: time alone with her. Time to hear that clear, bell-like laughter bubbling up from her slender throat to caress him like a lover's hand. A grudging smile twinkled in gray eyes as he returned her gaze. "What else makes you think that?"

"You've got to be a Scorpio! You haven't even bothered to tell me whether I'm right or wrong! But I've piqued your curiosity, haven't I?"

The waiter returned, and they ordered dinner. After he left, Taylor leaned forward questioningly.

"A salad and water? I can afford to buy you a steak, Katie, if that's what you want. You didn't have to order rabbit food."

"I don't eat heavy foods like meat this late at night, Taylor. Bad for your digestion. Your poor stomach will be up all night trying to digest the steak you just ordered."

"Is that the latest word on health foods?"

She unfolded the napkin, grinning. "You saw my bookstore. I devote a whole section to health foods."

"You're a health-food nut."

"I am not. I listen to my body, and it tells me what it wants to eat. Today has been so stressful that I haven't wanted—" She chewed on her lip, avoiding his sharp gaze.

"You haven't eaten all day?"

"Don't get angry! When I'm upset I get nauseated if I eat, that's all. So I don't eat."

Taylor felt another twinge of genuine concern. "You can't weigh over a hundred pounds soaking wet. You should have eaten, Katie."

She stared at him, lips petulant. "Just like a Scorpio— trying to control other people's lives."

"You can't tell me it's healthy not to eat all day," he droned.

"Everyone is different, Taylor. What do you do when you're upset? Raid the refrigerator?"

He rubbed his jaw in thought. "Yeah, usually. Eating helps calm me down."

"Well," she said, "you must have eaten your way through house and home last night."

He laughed. "You're pretty feisty aren't you?"

Katie couldn't resist a smile. "That was a cheap shot on my part. I'm sorry. So tell me, were you born in November?"

Taylor's eyes narrowed to slits. "How could you know that?"

"Scorpio lasts from October twentieth through November twenty-first. My intuition says you were born in November." She gave him a stern look. "Really, Taylor, I'm not clairvoyant, so quit looking at me like that! There are twelve signs in the Zodiac, and you're displaying all the symptoms of being a Scorpio. I have a one-in-twelve chance of being right. And those aren't high odds. It's simple logic, not psychic ability."

"I was born on November second. Happy?"

She scribbled the information on a piece of paper and placed it in her purse. "Very. Thank you."

"Well?"

"What?"

"Aren't you going to tell me all about myself?"

She shrugged. "Maybe."

"This isn't fair, you know. Using your knowledge of voodoo to find out about me."

"Voodoo! Taylor, good grief!"

"Then why do I feel as if I handed you the keys to my personality when I gave you my birthdate?"

Her fine eyebrows dipped dramatically. "For someone who doesn't believe in the metaphysical sciences, you're awfully upset about giving me some meaningless bit of information."

The waiter brought Taylor's drink, and he took a sip of the scotch on the rocks, studying her in the silence. "Are you always this impertinent?" he asked.

Katie's chagrin melted beneath his roughened tone. "Only with people like you who go around trying to prove that my world doesn't exist and only yours does."

"Then tell me about your world," he coaxed.

"Is this on or off the record?"

He lost his smile as he realized she hadn't forgotten for a moment that he was a reporter, that he had already damaged her reputation in his eagerness to get a story out. "Tonight is special. It's not business. I owe you an apology, Katie."

She sobered, running her slender finger around the pattern on the pale pink tablecloth. "All right," she whispered, looking at him through half-closed eyes, "I'll trust you, Taylor."

For some reason this made him angry. "Look, can't you just conduct polite dinner conversation—instead of baring your whole soul to me? It's dangerous, Katie. You could get taken advantage of."

"I don't indulge in small talk," she returned tightly, her eyes flashing. "Is that what you want from me? Is that what you're used to? Women who fill the air with shallow chatter?"

He clenched his teeth, glaring across the table at her. "And I thought *I* didn't know how to make light conversation," he said, his voice low. "You're worse than I am. In case no one has told you before, there is such a thing as pleasant social banter."

Her nostrils flared and she sat back, chin at an arrogant angle. "Don't tell me about social banter, Taylor Grant! If my honesty bothers you, let's part right now and call it a night. I can't get to know a man who runs away from intimacy."

Taylor stared at her in the icy chill. Intimacy. She had struck a raw nerve. "Intimacy means vulnerability," he said slowly. "And that spells disaster."

She snorted. "Baloney! I'm not afraid to allow people to get close to me. How can you expect any real human exchange if you don't open up to another person?" She was breathing hard, her breasts rising and falling beneath the muslin of the dress.

He shook his head disbelievingly. "Haven't you ever been hurt?"

Katie shoved her hands together beneath the table and gripped them tightly in her lap. "Sure I've been hurt. There isn't a human being alive who hasn't been. We're all hurting to some degree or another, Taylor. How we deal with our wounds is *our* choice. If you choose to hide behind walls, that's fine. But I choose to deal with my hurt differently. I won't put up walls to keep people away. I love life. I like waking up in the morning to see the dawn. And I love to walk in the hills of Rio Conchos at dusk to watch the sunset." Her voice dropped to a husky whisper. "And I like people. Why not look for the good in life instead of the bad?"

Taylor placed a rein on his anger. He picked up the fork, turning it slowly, mulling over her fervently spoken words. The silence thickened between them. Finally, he raised his head. His heart contracted with an unknown emotion as he drank in her peaceful face. Lord, how he longed for that serenity that seemed to emanate from Katie

Riordan like a beacon. "Tell me about yourself. I want to know how you've managed to survive for twenty-six years with this crazy philosophy of yours."

Her lips parted like ripe cherries. "I don't know if you're ready to hear about me and my lifestyle."

"Why don't you let me decide that?"

Katie chewed on her lower lip. "You and I are as different as night and day, Taylor. You're a realistic man who's been terribly wounded by someone or something . . . I sense your anguish. Why do you want to know about me? So you can tear me apart and feel assured that your way is best? Because if that's your motive, I don't want to tell you about myself."

Taylor reached out to claim her hand. He studied it: her fingernails were short and clean. He felt the small calluses on her palm. Working hands, he thought. Katie wasn't a hothouse flower in need of cosseting. No, clearly she worked hard. But her slender, graceful hands knew beauty, too. Was she an artist? A musician? He longed to feel those fingers on his body, touching him, making the pain go away. In her arms, Taylor knew he could find peace. And love . . . his eyes narrowed. Love? Where the hell did that word come from? Long ago he had concluded that there was no such thing as love. But Katie Riordan almost made him believe in it again. Eventually he allowed her to reclaim her hand, and he met her grave expression. Such a young face—yet there was an ageless wisdom in her deep blue eyes. They took his breath away . . .

"As foolish as this may sound, I want to know something about you because I'm searching for the missing parts and pieces of myself," Taylor admitted quietly. "Does that make sense?"

Katie nodded. "Yes. We all serve as mirrors for one another. In some way, in some form. What are you seeking, Taylor?"

"Peace of mind, maybe. I don't know."

"That comes from going inside yourself and confronting who and what you are. Or are not."

He scowled. "I'm not a very nice person on the inside, Katie."

"I don't believe that."

"Ask my ex-wife. She'll tell you what a coldhearted bastard I've been. I ruined our marriage. Pushed her into the arms of another man—"

"It takes two people to ruin a marriage, Taylor."

He shook his head, staring doggedly down at the fork in his hand. "Not in this case."

Katie blinked back sudden tears. If he saw her crying for him, Taylor would shut her out. The anguish she felt surrounding him made her want to reach out and take him in her arms—simply to hold him. To allow him that moment's reprieve from the guilt he was carrying around inside. And Katie sensed that he had allowed himself to be vulnerable with her, something he rarely did with anyone. Swallowing the tears, she leaned forward.

"Tell me about it," she said gently.

Taylor took an unsteady breath. "Not much to tell. I was one of the hottest journalists in New York City when I met Mary Ann. I had it all: fame, success, respect. I'd earned every shred of it. Most of it came from my reportage on the drug dealings in Manhattan. I did a piece on runaway kids who were being peddled on the streets, and it won me damn near every award in the field."

Katie bit down hard on her lower lip to stop from crying out. Taylor's voice had dropped to a roughened whisper when he spoke of these children. He was far more deeply affected than he would possibly admit. "The children?"

He nodded. "Yeah. The innocent kids whose biggest crime was to run away from home. The kids were picked up by pimps, shot up with heroin, and turned into mindless junkies."

"You must care for children a great deal."

He finally raised his head, his gray eyes dark. "I wanted a family and Mary Ann didn't. She was a fashion model, and she felt it would ruin her looks. And her career. She has the face and bone structure to keep modeling until she's in her forties. I guess I can't blame her for refusing. It's her body and she had a right to make the decision."

"And after you realized she didn't want children?"

Taylor stared down at the table. "Things fell apart over the next couple of years. Mary Ann took more modeling assignments, and I dug my own grave in the back streets of the city, covering the crime beat. I'd come home in the morning, sleep all day, and get up in the evening to work all night. Mary Ann said I never talked to her. And maybe I didn't. I found it hard to confide my deepest fears and wishes to someone whose deepest concern was a new wrinkle on her face."

Their meals came, interrupting the flow of intimacy that had built effortlessly between them. Taylor gave her a rueful look of apology.

"I didn't mean to bend your ear—tell you all my troubles. Tonight was supposed to be for you."

Katie smiled, picking at the salad, unable to force herself to eat much of it. She was still upset over the pain in Taylor's carefully modulated voice. "I consider it an honor to hear your troubles. I don't think you confide in many people."

He studied her in the dim light of the restaurant, entranced by her unique beauty. One moment she was a child. The next, a grave adult who looked as if she could not only carry the weight of the world on those small shoulders, but understand it fully as well. "You're magical, Katie."

She smiled warmly. "There's nothing magical about me, Taylor Grant. I'm simply human. Very human."

"And a very desirable woman," he murmured.

Heat flowed up into her face, and Katie demurely lowered her lashes, her heart beating wildly in her breast. "Thank you."

He frowned. "Aren't you going to eat? You've hardly touched that salad."

She gave a helpless shrug. "I'll be all right." And when she saw he didn't believe her she added, "Really."

"I've upset you, haven't I?"

Her blue eyes glimmered with tender regard. "No. If you stick around for any length of time, you'll soon learn that I'm easily touched by others. Maud calls me a cosmic barometer."

"Well," Taylor muttered, placing his fork on his plate, "I can't say knowing you has been boring. Not for one second."

A smile tugged at her lips. "And being a Scorpio, you're fascinated by people who make life stimulating."

Taylor grinned, as he placed his credit card on the table alongside the check. "That's true. I'm fascinated with the unusual; I enjoy digging until I get all the facts. I like to figure out why people run the way they do. And I intend to find out more about you."

"Is that a threat or a promise?"

Taylor smiled, rising after he had signed for the meal. "Take it any way you want," he murmured close to her ear as he helped her up from the chair.

A delicious shiver rippled down her back as Katie felt his warm breath against her cheek. His fingers were firm on her elbow as he escorted her from the restaurant into the darkness. It was a mild California night, and Katie looked up at the star-bright blanket of the night sky above them. "Look," she said softly, "isn't that beautiful?" She pointed upward with a slender hand.

Taylor slid his hand around her tiny waist, drawing her gently against him, craving her warmth, needing to feel her feminine softness against his male hardness. "Yes," he agreed quietly, "it is quite a spectacle."

Katie was wildly aware of him. Her heart took off at a thundering gallop. His movement to slip his hand around her and draw her close seemed natural, as if they had rehearsed it hundreds of times. "When I was a kid I used to lie on the grass at night and make up stories about the constellations."

Taylor gazed down at her upturned face, bathed with starlight. He was touched by the intimacy in her whispery voice. He inhaled her scent—it was lilac—mingled with the arousing natural perfume of her skin. "What kind of stories?"

Katie shrugged, allowed him to take her weight, enjoying this unexpected closeness. "For as long as I can remember, Mom used to read me Greek myths. And when I was about nine, I started reading some of her books on astronomy, the Zodiac, and mythology. It was a wonderful world of heroes and heroines, of bravery and courage in the face of adversity." She glanced up at him, smiling. "And sometimes there was a happy ending."

He shared her smile. She would make a wonderful mother, he thought, imagining Katie reading stories to her children. With her range of facial expressions and that haunting voice, she'd be an excellent reader. Just thinking about it sent a tingle of escalating desire through him; he wanted her to continue talking forever. "What else happened during those growing-up years of yours?" he coaxed.

Katie closed her eyes, savoring Taylor's throaty voice. It was as if he had leaned down and kissed her; his voice was a vibrating force that swayed her heightened emotions. "I loved watching cloud formations. I could see knights on horses, princesses in long, dazzling gowns, fierce dragons with huge wings, and turreted castles . . ." She sighed, fully relaxed against him, aware of his large, spare hand spanning her waist. "And thunderstorms! I love them. The first time I can remember wondering what the thunder was all about, I ran crying to my mother. She held me and asked me why I was crying. I remember sobbing, telling her that the sound scared me."

Taylor leaned down to rest his jaw against the fragrant silken mass of her hair. "And what did she tell you?"

"That a couple of giants were playing in the clouds, kicking tin cans around. And when they kicked the cans, it thundered." Katie gently eased herself away from him and turned to face him. Her midnight blue eyes were wide and luminous as she stared gravely up at Taylor. "And from then on, I looked forward to the next time that the giants would come to play. I always tried to catch them kicking the can."

Taylor lifted his hands, framing the perfect oval of her face, excruciatingly aware of the elastic velvet of her flesh beneath his fingers. "And did you, my magical lady who lives in her fairy-tale world?"

Her breath caught in her throat as he tipped her head up to meet his descending mouth. Katie anxiously examined his intent gray eyes, trying to ferret out the reason he wanted to kiss her. She ached to touch his sensual mouth, the mouth that so often drew in at the corners in pain. She longed to smooth those corners with her own lips and see him smile. What she saw in his hooded eyes made her blood turn to liquid fire while her lashes swept downward against her cheeks. His mouth barely brushed against hers, robbing her of all thought. Fingers tightening in demand, he drew her against his hard body. Her flesh tingled wildly as she felt his arousal. His mouth caressed her lips gently with small kisses meant to encourage her participation and not to frighten her. A moan of pleasure eased from her throat as he traced her parting lips with his tongue, sending rivers of molten desire flowing hotly through her trembling form.

"Katie," he groaned thickly, "open your mouth. Let me taste you . . ."

Mindlessly, she allowed his tongue entrance, her mind

exploding into a shattering state of pure pleasure that buck-
led her knees. She sagged against him, arms sliding upward, her fingers gripping the fabric of his shirt across his
broad chest.

And he was there, cradling her like a frail child, within
the protection of his arms. Gradually, he broke the spell of
the kiss, his face inches from hers. He stared darkly down
at her, mesmerized by the joy he saw in her vulnerable
face.. Her lips were glistening and pouty from his kiss,
open with invitation. He could feel the hardness of her
nipples pressed against his chest, the fluttering of her heart
against the heavier beat of his own. No woman had
drugged him into euphoria before. She was so small
against him, so breakable, and yet she trusted him completely. The kiss had shaken him deeply, and Taylor gently
pushed her away from him, seeing the confusion in her
eyes.

"I think we'd better get you home," he heard himself
say, his voice strained.

"All right . . ."

Taylor took a deep breath, gradually allowing her to
stand on her own. She seemed to sway slightly. "Katie?"

A slight smile curved her lips. "I'll be okay in a moment."

He stood, protecting her in the circle of his arms while
she reoriented herself. The dazed look in her eyes stunned
him. "I didn't realize I had such an effect on women."

"Oh," she whispered breathlessly, "you do."

His heart warmed to her honesty. He reached down,
brushing her fiery cheek with the back of his hand. "Are
you always so easily swept off your feet, sweetheart?" He
was afraid to hear her answer.

"No," Katie said.

Taylor laughed deeply, feeling a warm burst of pleasure.
"Come on, you must be cold." He placed his arm around
her shoulder, drawing her against him as they walked to-

ward the car in the distance. "You really are a child," he murmured more to himself than to her. "When I kissed you, it was as if it was your first time."

"I've never been kissed like that," she admitted huskily.

His spirits rose a notch further. "If any other woman said that, I'd doubt her. But not you." He smiled down at Katie. Her face was still filled with wonder. "I can see every one of your emotions. Did you know that, Katie? Your eyes are like cobalt mirrors. I can see in them exactly how you feel." Vividly he remembered the soft warmth of her mouth, hungrily matching his demanding kiss, sending a column of fire racing through him. No, she wasn't a hothouse rose: she was a lovely meadow violet—strong yet beautiful.

"You can?"

Taylor halted at the car, opening the door for her. "Yes."

"Oh."

"Nothing wrong with that. I like it."

She lifted her chin, staring deeply into his charcoal-gray eyes, silvered with simmering desire. "I'm glad. Do you know why?"

He shook his head. "No. Why?"

She reached out, barely grazing the corner of his mouth with her slender fingers. "Because you're smiling. At last."

Chapter 5

KATIE'S SENSE OF logic clashed with her emotions, each vying for supremacy as Taylor drove her back to her apartment above the bookstore. The look of tenderness on his face when she told him he was smiling had made her heart somersault with exquisite warmth. But another part of her whispered: He doesn't understand you. You're opposites. He knows nothing of what you believe in or what you do. Could he ever truly accept you? Despair washed over her at this point, and Katie chewed on her lip, staring sightlessly out the window. Taylor's world was one of harsh reality. Anything that couldn't be weighed, measured, seen with his own eyes did not exist. And yet, here they were, drawn to each other like iron chips to a magnet, these polar opposites . . .

Yet the part of him that attracted her was the part he so jealously hid from the world. Clearly Taylor had been badly hurt. He must have been, to be so unwilling to share his vast emotional reservoir. He had shared parts of it with her, only because she had remained vulnerable to him. Rubbing her head, willing away a burgeoning ache, Katie realized she didn't quite understand this new—and fragile —relationship.

Taylor glanced covertly at Katie. Her face was pensive, her eyes deep with thought. As he pulled into the parking lot behind the bookstore, he automatically scanned the shadowed recesses of the building, the spots that weren't illuminated by the streetlights.

"Come on," he murmured. "I'll walk you to your door."

They fell into step as they crossed the asphalt parking lot and walked into the shadows of the three-story brick building. Taylor waited patiently while she rummaged through every compartment of her purse in search of her key. A smile lingered on his mouth as he leaned against the doorjamb, watching her.

"Do you always have problems finding your keys?" he teased.

Frustration showed in the taut corners of Katie's mouth. "Oh, all the time! Maud says I should sew a key ring onto my purse. But somehow I haven't been willing to take such drastic action."

Taylor laughed softly. He reached out to run his hand lightly over her glorious ebony hair. It was soft, curly silk as he sifted it through his fingers. "You drop things, lose them, and bump into desks. You're a catastrophe just waiting to happen, Katie Riordan."

"And I've got the bruises to prove it," she muttered, thrilled by his caress. Finally, she found the keys, pulling them triumphantly from her purse. "There. Success!"

Taylor glanced at his watch. "Two minutes and forty-five seconds. Not bad," he drawled.

"Now, don't you start timing me. I'll be a nervous wreck, always trying to break my own record." She laughed, turning the key in the lock. Then she met his dove-gray gaze and melted beneath it. Taylor's face consisted of planes of darkness and light. Good and bad. Strong and weak. He mirrored for her in those poignant seconds what she had learned about herself over the years. No one was ever completely good or bad. And in Taylor's case, her heart whispered, he wasn't as hard-nosed as he appeared on the surface—or he wouldn't have been drawn to her openness in the first place.

"Listen," Taylor murmured huskily, breaking into her tailspinning thoughts, "I want you to be careful, Katie."

Her eyes widened momentarily as she caught the carefully veiled inflection in his low voice. Searching his face, she saw worry in his eyes. "Careful? Why, Taylor? I don't understand."

He grimaced, motioning to the shadowy darkness that surrounded them. "This is very poorly lit. Someone could jump you." He scowled. "How many threatening phone calls did you receive today?"

She shrugged. "A few."

"Katie . . ."

"All right, four."

"Same person or different ones?"

"I—I think it was the same man each time."

"That one who said he'd burn down your store?"

She nodded, chewing on her lower lip, touched by his concern. "I'm sure he's just some crackpot, Taylor. I'll be okay. The crime rate in Rio Conchos is very low, let me assure you. Even for a town of fifty thousand."

He crossed his arms over his chest, dissatisfied with her answer. "Now you listen to me carefully. I've spent seven years working with one of the best police departments in America. I've seen all kinds of crime, Katie, so take it from me: You can't just shrug off anonymous phone calls and insist that they're meaningless. I think you should call the police and—"

"Taylor, I told you; I'll deal with the threat in my own way. Trust me, please."

A glance at that ethereal face of hers failed to ease his mind. "How are you going to protect yourself, Katie? Pretend you didn't hear the caller's threats?" Frustration made his voice sound harsh.

"No. I have other ways to protect myself, Taylor," she insisted stubbornly.

"Not when I'm responsible for this whole mess."

"Please, let's not argue," she pleaded softly. Reaching out, Katie touched his arm, marveling at the steel-corded strength of his muscles. "We've had a wonderful two hours. Let's not spoil it by bickering."

He swallowed his building anger—and his fear. "Promise me one thing, Katie."

"Okay."

Taylor sighed impatiently. It was typical of Katie to agree before finding out what she was agreeing to. "If you get any more of those calls, I want you to call and tell me."

"All right, I will."

Taylor glanced up at the old brick building, realizing it must be close to a hundred years old. Probably a historical landmark of some kind. The mortar between the bricks had crumbled away in patches. Just how safe was the place? he wondered. He was sure it didn't meet the fire safety standards. He made a mental note to check all the records on the building tomorrow morning. Fear ate away at him when he realized there was no fire escape. If Katie was caught in her second-floor apartment, she would be trapped.

He placed his hands on her small shoulders, worry registering in his expression as he gazed down at her. At the moment, Katie appeared small and helpless. But he knew better; she had spunk, and the fervor of her personal beliefs gave her amazing strength—and stubbornness, he reminded himself sourly. "Just be careful," he said gruffly. "I don't want to lose you. Not so soon after I've found you."

She colored beneath his hungry look. "I'll be fine!" And then she sobered, stretching up on tiptoe. She rested her hands lightly on his chest and placed a kiss on his mouth. "Good night, Taylor. And thank you for a lovely evening."

Reluctantly he released her. "Sure, after I've spoiled the day for you."

"You've apologized. I don't need more than that."

His smile was grudging. "Somehow, apologizing didn't hurt as much as I thought it would. Good night, Katie. Dream of us . . ."

Katie lay awake for a long time. "Dream of us," Taylor had whispered. And every time she heard those words in the halls of her mind, her heart thudded intensifying the avalanche of emotions he had freed within her. In just that one soul-shattering kiss! Why was she so attracted to Taylor? He was a stranger to her; he knew so little of the real Katie Riordan. Worry threaded through the tumult of feelings. Turning on her side, Katie pulled the pale pink sheet over her shoulders and shut her eyes. Almost instantly, she slid over the abyss into sleep, into her own vivid world of nightly dreams where she loved to play. Only this time, her dark knight, Taylor Grant, was there at her side, laughing, smiling, loving her tenderly . . .

Katie's eyes widened as she unlocked the Unicorn Bookstore at ten o'clock the next morning. A horde of people bearing photographic equipment and television apparatus descended on her. Stunned, Katie was surrounded immediately. She had been awakened at five when the phone began to dance off the hook. Apparently that had been only the beginning! Helplessly, Katie looked up into the predatory faces of the men and women who were pushing and shoving to get closer to her. Panic set in, and she backed into a wall of books. Flashbulbs popped; the blinding light of several television cameras made her squint. Finally, she held up a hand to protect herself from the onslaught. Only one shred of coherent thought screamed through her stunned mind: Taylor! She had to reach Taylor. He would help her . . .

The phone rang shrilly, and Taylor glared at it. If he got one more phone call, he might just rip the cord out of the jack. He'd come to the office early—at seven—only to face a barrage of calls from reporters and newspaper editors from across the United States. Despite the cynical tone of his article, millions of readers were interested in Katie Riordan's miraculous ability . . .

"Hello," he snarled.

"Taylor?"

"Katie? What's wrong? What is it, sweetheart?" He straightened up in the chair, hearing the panic in her voice.

"It's awful, Taylor! There must be thirty reporters and four television news teams here in the bookstore. Please, I need your help. I don't want to answer their questions! I don't want the notoriety. Please, come over. I need you."

His gray eyes narrowed. "I'll be right there, princess. Just keep saying 'no comment' until I arrive. Do you understand me?"

"Y-yes," she stammered. "Please hurry. I feel like some kind of specimen being torn apart . . ."

As Taylor came through the door or the Unicorn, his eyes fell on an anguished Katie. She was surrounded by aggressive reporters. Swearing under his breath, he made his way through the mass of journalists until he stood before her. They had backed her up against the desk; her knuckles were white with tension as she gripped the edge of it. Her eyes were wide with confusion and blurred with unshed tears. He glared at the assembled reporters as his arm went around her shoulder to protect her. More flash bulbs popped. Video cameras whirred to life. And Taylor felt an anger more chilling than any he could recall. Katie glanced up at him.

"They won't listen to me, Taylor."

His hand tightened on her shoulder momentarily. "I will. What do you want me to do about this?"

"Just tell them to go away. I-I don't want to grant any interviews." Her voice was low and strained, and he could tell she was fighting to keep herself from crying in front of them.

"All of you," he roared above the chaos, "put down your cameras and turn off those damn videos. And give us some breathing room." His voice was deep with authority. Taylor divided his attention between the sullen news reporters and Katie.

"Hey! I'm from the *National Eagle*. I've been given the authority to offer Ms. Riordan ten thousand dollars for an exclusive on her story."

A tall red-haired woman elbowed her way to the front of the crowd. She glared at the reporter from the *Eagle*. "That smear sheet!" she snarled. Turning to Taylor, she shouted above the din, "I'm Louella Sharp from the *Daily World*, and I'll give Ms. Riordan *twelve* thousand for an exclusive on her magic touch!"

A third reporter shouted. "Fifteen thousand! I'm from the—"

"There will be no interviews," Grant said evenly, enunciating each word carefully. "You came stampeding in here like a herd of buffalo, and now you can stampede right back out."

"What's an exclusive, Taylor? Why are they offering me so much money?" Katie asked.

He gave her a suprised look, then shook his head. "They want to buy your exclusive story, Katie. If you take one of their offers, you'll be expected to tell everything to one paper. No one else gets an interview."

Katie stared at the wall of journalists and trembled. In misery, she lifted her chin. "Mr. Grant has the exclusive rights to my story," she said in firm, clear tones.

"I won't grant an interview to anyone else."

"But Ms. Riordan!" a television newsman protested, stalking forward with his cameraman, "you're an overnight sensation! Are you a witch? What are these powers you possess? The American public has a right to know!" He thrust the microphone into her face. Taylor promptly shoved it back at the reporter's chest.

"Ms. Riordan has a right to her privacy," he snarled. "Now, get your camera out of here before—"

"Please," Katie begged, "no fighting!" She looked over at the crestfallen reporter. "Mr. Grant has an exclusive. I won't talk to the rest of you. Please, just—"

"But surely you owe us—"

"She owes you *nothing*," Grant shouted. "Now get out of here before I have the police remove you bodily from the premises."

Katie hung her head, unable to take the collective glares and mutterings of the disappointed press. Taylor stood beside her, discouraging them from coming closer. He kept a hand on her shoulder, gently massaging, trying to make her relax as the reporters grudgingly turned and left the store.

"I'm sorry," he muttered. "I should have realized when the story went to the syndicate that half the world would be at your doorstep the next morning. Damn, I should have thought about that and warned you."

Katie raised her head, dashing away two tears that were threatening to fall. "It's all right. I started getting phone calls at five this morning. And when I opened the bookstore at ten they came inside in waves." She wrapped her arms round herself, trembling. "They were like jackals, Taylor."

He placed his hands on her shoulders. "Listen to me,

Katie. Did you mean it when you said you were giving me an exclusive?"

She gazed up into his craggy face. "Is that what you want?" Her voice was quiet and searching in tone.

Cursing softly, he gave her a small shake. "No, dammit! But you had to tell them something or they would have dogged your heels until you finally gave in and talked to them. So it was a smart thing to do—but did you mean it?"

She rubbed her eyes briefly, rubbing her temples. "Of course."

Taylor shook his head. "Look, I've done enough damage to you already, Katie. I wouldn't deliberately do it again. I'll be honored to take the exclusive on you. Like everybody else, I make mistakes, but I try not to repeat them."

Katie smiled. "I'm so glad you came, Taylor."

He gave her a tender look, then leaned down to kiss the tip of her nose. "Like a knight on a white horse riding to rescue the fair damsel in distress?"

Katie managed a small smile, still too shaken to think clearly. "Yes." She wanted to tell him that he stood head and shoulders above all the rest, that his strength had left her breathless. He had looked like a warrior, bursting through the doors, and she was grateful for his protection. "This is all such a shock, Taylor."

"Listen, Katie, we'll have to go ahead with this. If you don't give me that interview, the vultures will be back. They'll make life miserable for you." His eyes hardened as he watched her face drain of color. "They won't leave you alone until you break. And then they'll print only the sensational stuff. Half-truths padded with anything that will sell more copies of their papers at your expense."

She pushed herself away from the desk, and Taylor removed his hands from her shoulders. Walking aimlessly around the now quiet store, Katie tried to think. Finally, after stumbling over a pile of books that needed to be shelved, she scooped them up and turned to look at Taylor.

"When I gave you the exclusive, I was fairly certain you wouldn't print half-truths. Was I right to trust you?"

Taylor nodded, his face grave. "You'll have final approval on anything I write. Fair enough?"

A wan smile came to her lips. "Yes, that is fair."

"You'll have to give me the truth, though, Katie. *All* of it."

She slowly walked back to the desk, put the books down, and then straightened up. "I realize that."

"You have nothing to fear, Katie. You saved a man's life. The public won't burn you in effigy for that."

Sadness lingered in her blue eyes. "The public fears what it doesn't understand, Taylor. And I will be feared and misunderstood." She moistened her lips, her voice dropping to a haunting whisper. "You've seen just the tip of the iceberg. Half the phone calls are accusatory. The other half are congratulatory. It doesn't matter *what* they think, Taylor; they still won't understand me. And they still won't leave me alone."

Taylor couldn't understand the sadness in her. He wanted to reach out and comfort her, but he realized that holding her wouldn't help. No, the look in her eyes sent a bolt of fear through him as it slowly dawned on him that Katie Riordan was far more than he had bargained for. The phone rang, bringing them both back to reality. Without breaking eye contact with Katie, Taylor reached for the phone and answered it.

"Unicorn Bookstore," he snapped.

Katie watched Taylor's face cloud. Automatically she tensed.

"Who is this? Hey, don't hang up—damn!" He clenched his teeth, slamming the phone back into the cradle.

"Who was it?"

"Your friendly neighborhood arsonist. Something about making sure you wouldn't stay in Rio Conchos much longer. Hang on. I'm going to call the police."

Gooseflesh rose on her arms, and Katie turned away to hide the fear she knew showed on her face. Good Lord, what else could happen? No, she'd better not ask! Rubbing her arms, she wandered aimlessly around the bookstore, trying to collect her scattered thoughts. She was aware of Taylor's low voice, his tone lined with steel as he talked to the police. At last he hung up the phone.

"The deputy police chief will be here in a while. He wants to ask you a few questions, Katie."

"Oh, Taylor—"

"It's necessary. Whether you like it or not. How many times has that man called?"

She shrugged wearily. "I'd guess six times. This should be the seventh call."

"Is his voice at all familiar?"

"No."

Taylor watched Katie, and his heart wrenched. She looked incredibly pale and forlorn, standing in the cascade of sunlight pouring through the window. "My gut instinct tells me your caller means business, Katie. I don't want to alarm you, but you're going to need protection until the man is identified."

"What do you mean?"

"I don't think you should stay in the building alone at night."

Real fear began to suffuse her as she stared at him. Taylor was a police reporter, and she had to respect his evaluation of the situation. Would someone really try to scare her into leaving Rio Conchos—simply because she had laid her hands on a dying man? Was that justice? Katie felt the hot tears gather in her eyes. Then they were streaming down her cheeks . . .

"I won't leave, Taylor. I love my home. I need my

piano, my music—I need the peace and quiet that my home offers me."

"Get a hotel room for the next couple of days, Katie," he begged. "Just until the police nail this caller."

She shook her head. "I don't really have the money. I can barely make the mortgage payment each month, Taylor."

He cursed and walked toward her. "I'll pay for the hotel. I'm the one who's responsible for this mess. I'll foot *all* your bills."

He loomed so strong and confident before her. The moment he opened his arms to her, Katie entered his embrace. Exhausted, she rested her head on his chest, aware of the strength of his arms around her. Safe . . . she felt safe and cared for . . . and loved. The word seeped into her cartwheeling mind and found solace in her heart. It was more than mere guilt that pushed Taylor to help her, she realized. He could have walked away from her, and this whole business, but he hadn't. He had taken responsibility for his actions and moved to help her deal with the situation. And the tremor she detected in his carefully modulated voice told her of his feelings for her . . .

Katie gently dislodged herself from his arms, searching his worried face. "I want to stay here. I know it sounds crazy, Taylor, but my apartment is a sanctuary for me, a place where I can hide from the world. I love the colors I've chosen for it, the music I play there, and the peace it provides. Please try to understand. I live half of my life upstairs. The colors, the sounds, my plants—all are a part of me. That's where I feel safe and secure."

His mouth tightened into a firm line. "I can't persuade you to leave?"

"No."

His hands gripped her arms. "All right, then, I'll move in with you until this situation clears up. And no arguments, Katie. I'll sleep on the couch at night, so don't give me that panic-stricken look."

"But—"

"You're leaving me no choice, dammit! Now, listen to reason. You've got a dangerous sociopath out there, tormenting you for some twisted reasons. I got you into this, and I'll get you out of it. But you're going to have to trust me."

She searched gray eyes, fraught with frustration. "I don't know if my couch is long enough . . ."

Taylor managed a sour smile, relaxing his hold on her arms when he realized she wasn't going to fight him on that point. "So, I'll bring a sleeping bag. It doesn't matter."

"Yes, it does. You can have the bed. The couch is plenty big enough for me."

"I'll do whatever you want, Katie. Just allow me to help you, that's all."

Her heart was pounding erratically, and not from fear. Taylor Grant affected her senses like sunlight caressing flowers, flowers that turned their heads to follow the sun across the sky. With sudden certainty she knew Taylor's presence in her life signaled a transformation that was entirely new to her. "Why don't you bring whatever you need over, then?"

Taylor hesitated, watching as two customers walked through the door. "Okay. Sure you'll be all right here by yourself? I'd like to be here when the police arrive. We could get my things later."

Katie shook her head firmly. "Go on. You've got better things to do today than play watchdog."

He gave her a sharp look. "I'll guard you with my life, sweetheart. No one's going to harm you. I can promise you that."

Suddenly, all her anxiety about the forthcoming weeks melted away beneath his warm dove-gray gaze. Her world had been turned upside down, and her belief in herself had been severely tested. But it all looked far less threatening when Katie realized that Taylor Grant would be at her side throughout the ordeal that lay ahead. He might not know much about her, but she was beginning to learn that his integrity and his values were unquestionable. A silken thread of burgeoning love twined through her beating heart like a soothing balm . . .

Chapter 6

MAUD GAVE TAYLOR GRANT a disgruntled look when he sauntered into the Unicorn Bookstore, but she was too busy with a roomful of customers to do much else. Katie stood beside Maud, slipping the newly purchased books into plastic bags as her friend rang the purchases up.

"You know, at three o'clock five people are bringing in their animals for you to lay hands on," Maud groused just loud enough for Katie to hear.

"I know."

"You're pale, Katie. Are you up to it?"

Katie gave Maud a tender smile. "That's out of my hands, isn't it?"

"Humph, I 'spose so." Maud frowned darkly as she watched Taylor saunter to the back of the small desk area, winding his way through the chattering, smiling customers like a fox through sheep.

Katie felt some of her apprehension lift as Taylor shot her a brief smile. "Just a minute and I'll show you the way upstairs," she told him, thanking the customer. "Maud," she added, "I'll be right back."

"Fine, Katie."

Katie smoothed her floor-length purple skirt and re-tucked the shell-pink blouse. She straightened the red sash she wore around her slender waist, and wedging between the customers, hurried toward Taylor. Together they exited the bookstore, Taylor's hand firm on her elbow.

"Did the police come?" he asked.

"Yes, but they think I'm making the whole thing up, Taylor. I'm sure of it."

His eyes narrowed as he retrieved an overnight bag from the car. "But they will tap your line?"

She ran her fingers through her ebony hair, pushing it away from her face. "Yes, for the next seven days."

"That's all we want. I don't care whether they believe us or not. Okay, lead the way to this magical apartment that you refuse to leave, princess."

"It's my home! Don't you love to come home after a hard day's work at the office?" She led him up a darkened stairway that was set between two stores.

"What? Come home to an empty house?"

Katie heard the pain in his voice. At the top of the stairs she halted, inserted the key, and pushed open the door. "Well, for the next few days, I doubt you'll be lonely."

Taylor gave her an enigmatic look. Her fragrance enticed him; he yearned to reach out and take her in his arms. At that moment she appeared so vulnerable, so incapable of protecting herself . . . "Somehow, I agree with you," he murmured dryly, as he walked into her apartment.

He halted and looked around as Katie shut the door. The coolness provided by the air conditioning enveloped him, a shock after the eighty-degree heat on the street. He missed nothing in his inspection of the spacious apartment. The walls were painted a pale lavender. The drapes were of ivory lace, and through them the sun placed its muted pattern on the opposite wall. The carpet was a dusty rose, thick and luxurious beneath his feet. The furniture was bamboo, chairs and couches adorned with thick, wine-colored pillows that invited him to kick off his shoes, sit back, and relax. The multitude of greenery amazed him. It was as if they had stepped into a beautiful jungle. Chairs and a settee had been placed among the verdant splendor. Thick, luxuriant Boston ferns hung long, graceful arms near each of the three windows, while several palm and fig trees gave the living room a true breath of life.

Life, Taylor thought, as he looked around. The place had an amazing feeling of life about it. He could feel the energy, sense it. There was an unexplained joy and serenity in the room, and he halted, unable to pinpoint its exact source. And then, slowly, he turned his head to Katie, standing a few feet away. There was a knowing glint in her deep blue eyes.

And then he saw the grand piano in the corner. It was black lacquer and highly polished. Setting down his bag, he walked over to it and Katie followed.

"You said you played?" he asked.

"A little."

"Oh, I think more than just a little if you have a grand. I'll bet this instrument cost over ten thousand dollars."

Katie ran her hand lightly over the side of the piano, caressing it as if it were a living creature. "When my parents died unexpectedly, I inherited this piano. It was my mother's," she added in a wistful voice.

Taylor watched her expression, marveling at her ability to communicate so effectively with those eyes and that wonderfully soft mouth. "What happened to your parents?"

"They were coming out to celebrate the opening of my book shop five years ago. Their plane crashed on takeoff."

She took a deep breath. "It was a shock," she finished inaudibly, her eyes dark with memory.

"I'm so sorry, Katie. I'd like to have met your mother and father. They must have been very special people—to have created you." He wished he could soothe the anguish in her upturned eyes.

Katie sat on the piano bench. Gently she fingered the keys, bringing to life the soft notes of some unknown classic. Her slender fingers caressed the keys with delicate strokes, and Taylor found himself holding his breath. He wanted to capture the innate beauty of that instant. Then, as gently as Katie had brought the classic to life, she allowed it to flow back into the warming silence that surrounded them.

"My mother was a registered nurse, Taylor. And to combat the depression she often felt in dealing with terminally ill patients, she bought a piano to lift her spirits. I can remember when I was three years old, sitting on my mother's lap and plinking on the keys . . ."

He leaned against the piano, studying her closely. "And she taught you to play?"

Katie smiled, lost in those wonderful memories. "Yes. And when I was seven, they decided to give me formal lessons with a local teacher."

"Then why aren't you a concert pianist? You certainly play well enough."

She shrugged. "I gave it serious thought."

"But?"

Breaking into a smile, Katie rose. "I don't have the discipline. And to become a concert pianist, one had to be willing to devote his life. I loved the outdoors. I didn't want to be cooped up in a room playing a piano all day. Not when the sun was shining and the sky was a gorgeous dark blue. I wanted to be a part of that, too."

Taylor glanced around the living room. "Well," he

drawled, hiding his own smile, "I'd say you brought the outdoors in to live with you." He noticed vases of wild-flowers from the surrounding hills of Rio Conchos: one rested on the mahogany stereo; another stood in colorful profusion on the bamboo and glass coffee table in the center of the room. Plum, crimson, and cerulean blue pillows were thrown casually about the coffee table, giving the room a Japanese cast.

"I eat my dinner there," she explained, pointing down to the coffee table.

"You eat you meals in the living room? Off the floor?"

Her grin was infectious as Katie beckoned him to follow her. "The coffee table is my official dining area. I may be a klutz, but I manage not to scatter my food on the floor. Come on, you'll see why the living room has to double as my dining room."

The apartment had obviously been converted from an office into a living area, Taylor thought. The kitchen was exceedingly narrow, offering just enough room for one person to move around. She was right: there was no place for a table and chairs. The area was flooded with sunlight. Several philodendrons in wicker baskets hung from the ceiling. Brightly colored wallpaper adorned one wall, lending the kitchen an old-fashioned feeling that Taylor thoroughly enjoyed. And never mind its lack of size!

"As you can see, this place wasn't that well designed," Katie said, leading him into the bedroom and the adjoining bathroom.

"It's beautiful," Taylor said somberly. "Just like you are."

"Well—thank you," she murmured.

He longed to reach out and wind those raven strands of gently curling hair around his fingers. Today Katie had gathered it up at the crown of her head. A plum-colored ribbon tamed it and kept it from her face, leaving only a fringe of wispy bands across her brow. "You improve everything you touch, Katie. Look what you did to this place."

It was true: the bedroom was a brilliant, lively green; the drapes were jade with beige and orange flowers. Above the double bed, covered by a spread that matched the drapes, Katie had hung apple-green chiffon netting. The atmosphere shouted of the Arabian Nights. Taylor grinned down at her.

"Katie, has anyone ever told you that you live out your fantasies?"

She returned the grin. "A few people have, yes. But why not?" She gestured gracefully with her arm. "My home is my castle. I feel safe here. I love the colors, the plants. And when I play my piano, the whole place vibrates with such incredible joy that sometimes I cry."

His smile widened as he luxuriated in that very sense of happiness surrounding her. "Will you play for me some night, princess? I could use a few moments of joy."

Katie sobered. "I know exactly what I'm going to play for you. I'm going to draw you out of that shell you hide behind, Taylor Grant."

Laughing, he brushed her cheek with the back of his hand. Her skin was pliant and yielding beneath his touch. "This is incredible. You're incredible," he whispered, his eyes darkening. And, he wanted to add, magical. There *was* something magical about Katie Riordan. For a second, Taylor had the feeling she was so special that she didn't belong there. It shook him with a momentary panic. There was an inscrutable secret in Katie that he hungered to understand and become a part of. She exuded a serenity and peace that had eluded him thus far in life. And just being around her allowed him to relax and be himself more than he could recall ever having been . . .

"Let me put my stuff in the bathroom, and then we'll go downstairs," he heard himself say. Lord, he wanted to do anything *but* that! He wanted to lift Katie in his arms, carry her to that sumptuous bed strewn with pillows, and make passionate love to her. A charged excitement sparked between them in that instant and it took every fiber of strength in Taylor Grant to pull away from her. Did Katie know what she was doing to him? Turning him inside out with a burning hunger to make her his own? Did Katie realize that her slightly parted lips gave her a breathless vulnerability that made him want to protect her? That her lapis lazuli eyes, deepened by the black fringe of lashes, pulled him into their hypnotic depths? He wanted to lose himself in the yielding warmth of her feminine body. He wanted to rest his head against her breasts and allow her just to hold him. Taylor craved everything about her. Whatever she might be. It didn't matter what secret she carried within her, he thought, setting his bag down in the bathroom. No matter what Katie told him about herself, it wouldn't deter him from exploring, enjoying, drinking in all aspects of her delightfully enigmatic personality. . .

Katie glanced at her watch; it was almost three. She shut her eyes, wishing this tiring day were over. It hadn't been easy. Several reporters returned to badger her into giving them a story. Maud drew up into her fiercest stance and finally shooed them out the store just as Taylor returned from a brief errand.

Taylor glared at the reporters trooping out into the hot afternoon sunlight. Maud wagged her finger at him as he halted by the desk.

"This is all your fault, you know, Mr. Grant! Those reporters are like jackals and they practically drove Katie to tears. You ought to be ashamed of yourself!"

"Maud, it's all right," Katie soothed, managing a wan smile for Taylor's benefit. "Come on, I have to get the back room set up for our patients. They'll be arriving soon. Taylor, are you coming?"

He nodded and decided not to say anything to Maud. She was right: He had started this whole business. He followed Katie into the next room. It turned out to be a classroom with desks, a lectern at the front, and a huge chalkboard. With Taylor's help, Katie pulled out a small table.

"What's going on?"

Katie went to the washroom in back and scrubbed her hands with soap. "People bring their sick animals every day at three so I can lay hands on them," she explained. Picking up the towel, she dried her fingers and then joined him.

He frowned. "Laying hands on? Like you did with Joe Collins?"

"Yes. Exactly the same."

Taylor crossed his arms over his chest. He watched as Katie picked up a piece of chalk and drew a human form on the board. "You're an artist, too."

"A poor one, believe me. Okay, lesson number one in metaphysics, Taylor. Around everything organic and inorganic there is an energy field. It's electromagnetic—or, put more simply, it's like an electrical field around us. Metaphysicians call it the aura." She chalked an outline around the human figure she had drawn. "This first field is known as the etheric. And if you unfocus your eyes and look past my shoulder as I stand against this blackboard, you'll be able to see a clear outline of my body—it should appear shaped like a colorless blanket, following its shape." She turned to him and stood still. "Want to try it?"

He grimaced. "Come on, Katie . . ."

Her eyes flashed. "Unfocus your eyes," she insisted. "It isn't any big deal to see the etheric aura. Anyone can. It won't shock or scare you. All you're doing is using your eyes to 'see' one of the electrical fields that surround all of us."

Grudgingly, Taylor unfocused his eyes. His brows

dipped and after a few seconds, he shook his head. "I can't see a thing, Katie."

"That's to be expected at first. But if you were more relaxed, you would. You were trying too hard."

His mouth became a grim line. "I don't believe in what I can't see," he said stubbornly.

"Fair enough. But keep an open mind for a few more minutes while I review the mechanics, will you? Because then, when I lay hands on the animals, you'll realize what is happening. It isn't magic or any such nonsense." Now she drew an eggshell shape around the human figure on the chalkboard. "This next field is called the astral body. It's our emotional body, Taylor. And it changes color according to our moods." She drew several other oval shapes outside the two she'd already drawn. "These are known as the mental and causal fields; I'm not going to explain them at this point, because it gets quite complicated. Suffice it to say, Taylor, there is more to us than meets the naked eye." She laid the chalk down and faced him with her hands raised.

"We can use a technique known as Kirlian photography to take pictures of our etheric field. They show the energy coming off our bodies as a luminescent pattern. I have several books on the subject, if you'd care to take a look."

"Oh, I will, rest assured," he added quietly. "Go on, you've managed to rouse my curiosity."

Katie smiled, spreading her fingers. "All right, we are all in our own electrical field. When I lay hands on another, whether it's a human or an animal, there is a meeting and blending of energies."

"Sparks don't fly?" he queried, grinning.

Katie laughed like a delighted child, clapping her hands. "In some cases, that actually happens. But most people just feel a magnetic attraction to each other. They can't see it or touch it, but they perceive it. And what they are perceiving is the field around another individual." Her eyes glinted with humor. "And in some cases, when this occurs, there is instant love, hate, trust, or distrust." She shrugged. "When you asked me to help you with Joe Collins, and I knelt across from you, I immediately felt protected in your presence, Taylor. You make me feel safe."

"That's all?"

She blushed. "What do you feel when you're around me?" she countered.

Taylor grinned, letting his arms relax and fall to his sides. "That, princess, is a leading question."

"It wasn't meant to be," she said, flustered.

That same catlike smile creased the corners of his sensual mouth as he studied her. "What I feel toward you shouldn't be put into words. If I were to do that, I'm sure you'd turn red as a beet."

Nervously, Katie chewed on her lower lip. "Let's stay off the physical for a few minutes more, okay? I need to explain what happened when I touched Joe Collins."

Taylor nodded and seated himself on the edge of the desk next to her. "First I have to believe that we all have this electrical field around us—"

"That can be proven with the use of the Kirlian photography."

"Okay. What next, professor?"

Taylor was too close. And too sensual! Heart pounding, Katie moved off of the desk to draw another picture on the board. This time she sketched a prostrate form, with another form kneeling beside it. "This is the part I can't prove to you. You'll just have to take my word for it, Taylor. I'm sure that as Kirlian photography is refined over the next few years, we'll be able to actually see healing take place."

"Healing? As in faith healing?"

Katie gave him a thoughtful look. Should she go into the specifics? Finally, she bowed to her intuition and threw caution to the wind. "My mother, Ruth, as I just told you, was a nurse. She noticed that when she touched her patients, her hands would become exceedingly warm—even hot. And her patients mentioned this to her, too. But the most interesting result was that after my mother touched a patient—even for a minute or so—he felt better afterward."

Taylor crossed his arms, scowling. "In what way, Katie?"

"The patients perked up, had more energy, and entered a better frame of mind."

"And you have this same gift?"

"It's not really a gift. Anyone can do it."

"I see. So when did you become aware that you had this talent . . . ?"

"After many years, my mother decided to find out exactly why her touch affected her patients so positively. That was when she delved into metaphysics and began to investigate various theories. She learned that many Eastern philosophies embrace the theory I've just drawn for you on this chalkboard. And when I was nine years old, my mother began to teach me the fundamentals of metaphysics, too."

"Why?"

"Because whenever I got sick as a child, my mother would lay her hands on me and heal me. I was absolutely fascinated with the idea that the laying on of hands could help others. And so, when I was nine, I laid hands on Tommy, my next door neighbor. We had been playing in an old gravel quarry. Tommy fell off his bike and tore up his knee. He was lying there, the bent and twisted bike wheel pinning his leg. I was distraught. When I tried to move him, he screamed in pain. We were too far away to get help, and we weren't supposed to be in the quarry anyway. I knelt down and put my hands on his leg. And I concentrated on helping him. My hands got hot. Tommy quit crying, and we just stared at each other because he could feel it, too."

"Feel what?" Taylor demanded.

"The heat and the other sensations that accompany the healing energy that flow through me," she explained simply, trying to decide whether Taylor was going to laugh openly or retain that deadpan expression.

"Show me."

Without hesitation, Katie placed her hands on his outstretched arm.

Taylor was aware of how lightly her hand touched his flesh. Almost immediately, he became conscious of an intense heat flowing from her hand. And then a decided tingling sensation traveled through his arm and up into his shoulder. His eyes widened momentarily. Katie's gaze was unwavering and serious.

"You feel it, don't you?"

His mouth tightened. "It must be because I'm holding my arm out. That's placing unusual stress on the muscles in the shoulder," he muttered, breaking contact with Katie.

"It isn't."

He rubbed his forearm where the tingling persisted. Katie clapped her hands sharply and then shook them at her sides. "What was that for?" he asked.

"To dispel any energy that lingered on my hands. It's similar to when a doctor washes his hands after surgery. In a few minutes, when I work on the animals, you'll see me do it after every healing."

Taylor remained silent, watching her. Disbelief mingled with shock. "Why didn't you defend yourself when I challenged you just now?"

Katie lifted her chin. "The truth needs no defense. I am what I am. Nothing more, nothing less. I have no need to prove myself to anyone, Taylor. What's important is that *I* know it works. If I can provide relief to those who experience pain and suffering, that's all that is important to me."

Taylor was moved by her sincerity. She decidedly was the most complex human being he had ever met! Staring down at her delicate artistic hands, he shook his head.

"I warned you Taylor," Katie said softly, "that once it becomes widely known that I can heal, there will be fear and misunderstanding. And the greatest sadness is that since healing works, since it helps alleviate suffering, why should people be frightened of it? It's fear of the unknown, Taylor. Fear of that which can't be easily understood. And that fear will put my life under inquisition . . ."

Chapter 7

GRUDGINGLY TAYLOR ADMITTED that Katie was right. Five people arrived with ailing pets. They sat quietly at the desks. One at a time, Katie called them up with their animal. Taylor sat back, arms crossed over his chest, watching.

The first to stand was a woman near ninety. She carried a scruffy gray cat which looked to be the same age. Katie's face broke into a welcoming smile as she took the cat into her arms.

"How's General this week, Mrs. Beaumont?"

"Just grand, Katie. Why, I've even taken him off the kidney medicine."

Katie sat on the edge of the desk and stroked the gray tomcat. "With Dr. Abram's permission?"

Mrs. Beaumont nodded, touching the pin that held her black hat at a jaunty angle on her silver hair. "I asked him—just like you told me." A beatific smile spread over her wrinkled face. "General's eating now, thanks to you!"

"And to Dr. Abrams," Katie reminded her, smiling. She held the cat for about a minute before handing him back to his owner. "I think that's all he needs for now."

"May I bring him next week?"

"Will you feel up to it, Mrs. Beaumont? I can always walk down the street and visit if it gets to be too much—"

Mrs. Beaumont patted Katie's hands, now resting in her lap. "Just give me a touch and I'll make it back," she said, her blue eyes twinkling.

Katie laughed, placing a hand on Mrs. Beaumont's arm. "You've got some color in your cheeks, Mrs. Beaumont."

"Thanks to you, young lady. I can remember when I was a child, Dr. William Adams used to ride up on his old mule, Henry. I had a fever, Katie. Only the Lord's will— through Dr. Adam's healing touch—kept me alive. We all looked forward to the laying on of his hands, when we were sickly." She smiled. "Hands like yours. Hot when they touched you. And afterward, that tingling sensation that flowed through your body, making you feel so much better, everywhere . . ."

Katie turned her head to gauge Taylor's reaction. His eyes were narrowed to near slits, his mouth pursed into a thin line. He was fighting her then, fighting what and who she was. Well, what did she expect? Returning her attention to Mrs. Beaumont, she squeezed the old woman's arm, then released her. "You're in great shape. I'll see you next week."

The next visitor was a slender boy of ten, a small cage gripped tightly in his arms.

"Hi, my name's Katie. What's yours?" she asked, leaning over and touching the boy's silky brown hair.

"Brandon Prater, Miss—"

Her smile broadened. "Call me Katie. May I call you Brandon?"

His downcast face brightened slightly. "Sure." He held out the small cage. "My friends say you can help sick animals."

Katie gently wrested the cage from Brandon's small, protective hands. She placed it in her lap. "I try to, Brandon. What have we here? A gerbil? What a pretty color. I'll bet you have a name for her?"

Brandon's face took on a look of hope. "Her name's Suzie."

Katie studied the gerbil, which looked like a tiny, distended balloon. "Pretty name. What's wrong with Suzie?"

The boy stuffed his hands into his trousers pockets, shrugging. "Suzie just keeps getting fatter and fatter, Katie. Mom thinks she might have a tumor or something." His hazel eyes gleamed with tears that he refused to allow to fall. "She's my friend, Katie. I saved all the money I got from collecting aluminum cans to buy her and her cage. And now. . ." He took such a deep, adult breath into that slight body.

"Mom thinks Suzie's dying," the boy continued. " 'Cause she's getting so big so fast. And I don't overfeed her." His face turned earnest. "They said you could help when no one else could. That's why I brought Suzie. Please, I love my pet. She sits on my desk every night when I do my schoolwork and keeps me company."

"I see," Katie murmured, opening the cage and sliding her fingers beneath the rotund and sluggish Suzie. Picking the gerbil up, she studied it intently. Her blue eyes sparkled with repressed laughter.

"How long ago did you buy Suzie?"

"About two weeks."

Katie held Suzie in the palm of her hand, so the gerbil was at eye level with Brandon. "And in the pet store was Suzie in a cage with boy as well as girl gerbils?"

Brandon nodded. "Yeah, they had a whole bunch of them together. I picked her because she was the prettiest."

Katie lifted her chin, meeting Taylor's gray gaze with a smile. Then she turned back to Brandon. "I don't think Suzie is sick, after all."

"No? Honest?"

"Honest. I believe she's pregnant, honey. No tumors. Just lots of little babies that Suzie's carrying inside of her. I'll bet she'll have them any day now."

Brandon's face lit up. "Really? Babies? Suzie isn't going to die?"

Katie maintained a serious expression, gently depositing the decidedly pregnant Suzie back into the nest of wood chips in the bottom of the cage. "Your mother is in for a shock, but I'm sure it'll all end happily." She returned the cage to Brandon who now handled it even more tenderly. The act brought a smile to Katie's face. "Just make sure Suzie gets lots of greens. Throw in a few dandelions from time to time and you'll have a bunch of healthy baby gerbils on your hands."

"Gosh, thanks, Katie!" Brandon dug furiously in his jeans pocket. Producing three quarters, he held them out to her. "This is all I have, but if you—"

Katie took his hand and closed it around the coins. "There's no charge for what I do, Brandon. Besides, I didn't do anything!"

Brandon was crestfallen. "You did plenty. Suzie isn't going to die. Mom said that if I took the responsibility of buying Suzie, then I should pay all her bills, too."

Leaning over, Katie placed a kiss on his hair. "Normally, I'd agree with your mother. But all I did was diagnose Suzie's condition. And even if she did need a healing, I wouldn't charge, Brandon."

"Why?"

"Because it wouldn't be right. That would be like God charging us for breathing the air. Or sending us a bill for the use of gravity. Would that be right?"

Brandon shook his head, perplexed. "No . . ."

"You can't put a price on love," she told him seriously.

* * *

Taylor asked the last three people if he could take photographs while Katie treated their animals. All agreed. It took Katie less than half an hour to finish with her ailing charges. Everyone thanked her profusely. Taylor sauntered back toward the sink where Katie was washing her hands.

"My, you look serious, Taylor. Which are you: frightened, defensive, or confused?" Her heart leaped as he leaned over without warning and pressed a light kiss on her parted lips.

"None of the above, princess," he murmured, walking beside her to the front of the classroom. He put his arms around her, marveling at how small she was—and yet how strong and loving. "I'm deeply touched by your ability to help these people and their pets," he began slowly, searching her upturned face. Dark smudges had begun to show beneath her lovely eyes. The last few days had been hard on her, he realized. Katie didn't deal with certain types of stress very well. But then, he told himself, if someone were trying to expose *him* to the world, he'd be stressed, too.

"I wanted to be a veterinarian for a while," she admitted, disturbingly aware that mere inches separated them. He made her feel feminine, made her long to be womanly for him alone. She smiled softly. There was a charisma about Taylor Grant, one that drew her effortlessly to him . . .

"What stopped you?" he asked, trailing a finger down the velvet slope of her cheek.

"I couldn't stand biology." She flinched slightly. "It was all those experiments. I can't stand the sight of blood. I—uh, well, I faint."

"I'd believe that."

She gave him a dark look.

"Because, princess, you're overly sensitive to everything." And then he scowled. "And to everyone." He thought of the threatening phone call—as he did almost once an hour whether he wanted to or not.

Katie reached up to rest her hands on his well-muscled arms, aware of their controlled strength. "People like me do tend to be sensitized to everything," she agreed. "We feel things more intensely, perhaps, than most."

He cocked his head, studying her guileless face. "I saw the tenderness in your eye when you were working with Brandon."

"He's a wonderful little boy," she said, "so manly. He was trying so hard not to cry—all out of worry over his gerbil. I was touched by it, Taylor."

"So was I. By both of you."

Katie tilted her head, her luminous eyes sparkling. "That's nice to hear. I know you feel things deeply, too, but you rarely allow those feelings to surface. Nor do you share that side of yourself with anyone."

"It's you," he accused, leaning down to taste her lips. "You," he repeated against their pliant sweetness. "You reach out and touch the world, and you wear your heart on your sleeve." He molded his mouth against hers, feeling her body against him, graceful as a willow. He claimed her gently, as if she were a priceless, fragile gift. There was melting fire in her returning ardor, and he was aware of her strength as well as her weaknesses. And Taylor could sense that where she was weak, he could be strong for her. An even more disturbing discovery was that Katie could be strong in those areas where he was weak.

Reluctantly, Taylor drew away, his eyes silver with passion. Her lips were full and petulant, begging to be kissed again. And the lilac fragrance mingled with the scent of her warm, willing body, made him almost dizzy with need. "Lord," he groaned, crushing her against him, "you feel good, taste good . . ."

Katie smiled languorously, allowing him to hold her. "So do you." She sighed softly, barely able to think coherently. Her body flamed, her knees felt wobbly, and she didn't trust herself to walk without support. So she simply rested against his hard length, listening to the powerful beat of his heart while she recovered. "Leave it to a Scorpio man to be the world's greatest kisser." She sighed.

Taylor laughed softly, nuzzling his face into the silken folds of her hair. "Another generalization about Scorpio males?"

"Well—Scorpio's a water sign, and Scorpio men can communicate well on the emotional level—if they want to."

"I like communicating this way."

"Every Scorpio male does."

He grinned down at her. "You mean we're passionate?"

Katie drew slowly away, meeting his taunting smile. "Scorpios have a corner on *that* particular market," she warned.

Taylor shrugged. "It can't be all that bad, if you enjoyed it."

"I enjoyed it," she told him huskily.

Deviltry lurked in his gray eyes. "On a scale of one to ten, how did it rate?"

She laughed throatily, leaving his embrace. "Oh, no! I'm not going to be responsible for swelling your head any more than it already is. You and I aren't children. We know how we affect each other."

Taylor shot her a playful look. "I think I just got an eleven."

"You're impossible!"

"Yeah, so I've been told."

She eyed him, enjoying their renewed intimacy. He had been hurt by a woman, her instincts told her. And he needed to know how deeply he affected her. It would do his wounded ego good to find that not all women were out to destroy his manhood. But Katie kept these thoughts to herself, rewarding him with a dazzling smile.

"Come on," she said, "I have to relieve Maud. She'll want to get some dinner. We don't close till eight tonight. Remember?"

"The only thing I remember is your warm body next to mine, your soft, hungry lips—"

"Taylor!"

He grinned, watching a flush paint her cheeks fiery pink. "I'm just communicating my emotions."

"You Scorpios!" she said. "You're all alike!"

Taylor busied himself at the desk, writing down some notes of what he had seen earlier, while Katie forced herself to go through several boxes of newly arrived books. Deep in thought, he raised his head and watched her. Katie struggled silently with the list in her lap as she sat on the floor, completely surrounded by books. A slight smile crossed Taylor's mouth. Her brows were drawn together in concentration as she checked the book order, her mouth pouty. Did she realize how delicious she was? And then he laughed to himself. Maybe Katie was right. He had passion on the brain. But it rose in direct response to Katie Riordan, and no other.

Idly he sat back in the creaky chair, enjoying the stolen moment. Since Maud's departure at five, customer traffic had dropped to a minimum. "Want to take a break?" he asked. "I've got some questions for you."

"Am I glad you asked! I hate doing this detail work!" She sprang to her feet, smiling, and brushed the wrinkles from her skirt.

"You looked in need of rescuing," Taylor murmured dryly.

"You should hire someone who *enjoys* detail work."

"What I need is a Virgo. They're great at organization," she muttered.

"What are you, anyway?"

"A Sagittarian."

"Ah, the centaur. Running around with his bow and arrow." Taylor nodded sagely, holding her gaze. "That suits you: galloping off half cocked, tilting at windmills like Don Quixote."

Katie smiled. "Sagittarians like to travel. They like to stay in a state of constant motion. And they love their freedom."

"Is that why you're not married?"

The laughter left her face. Sitting down at the desk, she said, "No."

Clearly he had struck a nerve. But the detective in him demanded to know more. "Why not, Katie? You're certainly pretty enough. Great sense of humor. Nice body."

She tried to rally to his gentle teasing and pull herself out of the sudden tailspin of depression. "I was engaged once . . . quite a while ago. I made a fatal mistake when I was twenty-two."

"What? Falling in love?"

"No. When I met Wes I neglected to tell him about my healing ability." She chewed on her lower lip for a moment. "I thought nothing of it, but he did."

"I don't understand."

She turned her head, staring at him intently. "This afternoon I watched you closely, Taylor. I saw the outright disbelief on your face. And, yes, I saw your fear and then your confusion." She held up her hands. "I've met very few people outside the field who can accept what I am and what I do. And when I told Wes about it, he flipped out. He thought I was crazy. He thought I should see a therapist."

"He was unable to accept your healing abilities?"

"Yes. And I couldn't marry him if he couldn't accept that." Her voice showed her pain. "He called me an oddity. And he treated me as if I had leprosy or something."

"Katie, you have to admit that you're very different from most people."

She gazed at him sadly. "But what you don't understand is that there are hundreds of thousands of people all over the world who have the same abilities as I do. Only we don't go around talking about it, because most people would be frightened. We aren't a secret organization. We willingly share what we know when asked. Healers have been around since the dawn of time, Taylor. And I'm not much different from anyone else. I have a heart that feels, eyes that see. I'm human... only that. Nothing more, nothing less."

He was shaken by the pain in her voice. "I'm beginning to understand why you shy away from publicity, Katie," he admitted quietly. "Wes wasn't the only one who called you an oddity, was he?"

Katie closed her eyes and shook her head. "No. From the time I was nine years old, I've learned—the hard way—to say nothing about my healing. And I can't remember how many times I ran home from school to cry in my mother's arms because the other children were afraid of me." She opened her blue eyes, which were now awash with tears. "I'm a healer, just as you're a writer. Do I condemn you because you have writing talent? Isn't that an unexplained skill? Isn't musical ability? Isn't artistic talent? I only wish that healers could be as easily accepted as writers, musicians, and artists. All we want to do is be of service to our fellow human beings." Katie clasped her hands and bowed her head. "I want to fall in love with a man who will accept me as I am. I want children. I want what everyone wants: just a small portion of happiness..."

Taylor roused himself, trying to find words that would soothe her, but discovering none. "Look, Katie, don't you think it's time you—or someone like you—took a stand? Showed the world what you have to offer?"

She ran her fingers through her hair. "I've thought about that, Taylor. But you'll find that most healers are modest, shy people who can't take the glare of publicity." She gave him a meaningful look.

"And I was a real barracuda, wasn't I?" he said ruefully.

"Now you understand why I begged you not to print that story." She shrugged. "And I was right, too. What has it gotten me besides threatening phone calls, people coming here to stare at me as if I were an exhibit on display, and harassment by reporters from trashy newspapers and magazines who want to exploit me?" Katie got up, pressing her fingers to her temples, willing away a headache. Maud returned just then, making it impossible to continue the conversation. Taylor grimaced and looked down at his notes. Perhaps, somehow, he could make amends.

"First things first," Katie told Taylor as they entered her apartment. "I'm going to soak in a hot bath. I'm so exhausted!"

Taylor nodded, shutting the door. "Go ahead. I'll rummage around in the refrigerator and get us something to eat."

Katie hesitated at the bedroom door. "Give me fifteen minutes and I'll make us dinner."

"Okay."

She gestured toward the spacious living room. "Kick off your shoes and make yourself comfortable. There's wine in the refrigerator."

"Sounds good. Want some?"

Katie laughed ruefully. "Tired as I am, one glass of wine would send me under the table. No thanks."

She hadn't meant to fall asleep in the bathtub filled with orange-scented crystals, but she had. The past few days had been hard on her emotionally, and at night her sleep had been punctuated by worry. She had greeted each new morning with bloodshot eyes. Now, immersed in the fragrant hot water, her eyes dropped closed and she relaxed completely. Katie heard a noise in the small bathroom, but opted to remain in that in-between state, desperately wanting to sleep. She felt strong, gentle hands sliding up her rib cage, settling beneath her arms, and lifting her up . . . up and out of the lukewarm water. Her lashes opened drowsily. Taylor's worried face danced before hers.

"Just relax, princess," he murmured gruffly as he wrapped her in a fluffy pink towel. He dried her gently, then reached for her lavender silk robe.

"What happened?" she mumbled.

"Nothing. I got worried when you'd been in here forty-five minutes. You fell asleep in the tub, Katie." He smiled tenderly, ignoring her protest as he wrapped the robe around her soft, naked body and drew the belt tight around her waist, tying it awkwardly. "Come on, you're going to bed."

Her mind wasn't functioning at all, and Katie groped to resist his arm as he led her into the darkened bedroom. "But—"

"Shh, you need sleep, Katie. You're worn out. Now, come on, slip under the covers . . ."

Her heart pumped noisily in her breast as he lifted her off her feet and into his arms. She was aware of his provocative male scent, of his potent masculinity. She was safe, her heart whispered. Releasing a sigh, Katie slid her arms around Taylor's neck, resting her head wearily against his shoulder.

"Thank you," she murmured.

Taylor laid her on the bed, drawing the sheet over her. Moonlight gleamed through the latticework of drapes, giving the room a molten glow. "Go to sleep, princess," he urged, leaning over her to caress her hair.

Her thick lashes rested against her cheeks as she snuggled into the downy pillow. "You're a true knight," she whispered, her voice trailing off into sleep.

Taylor watched her sink into the arms of slumber. She

was so small she seemed little more than a child in the huge bed. And she looked even more beautiful in sleep, if that was possible. With her lips slightly parted, a slender hand curled near her head, moonlight cascading over her quiet form, she was like an ethereal dream . . . Shaking his head, Taylor wondered if he had fallen under a magical spell. He had experienced feelings and emotions that he'd thought were long dead and buried. Were Katie's simplicity and honesty the keys to a rebirth of sorts—another chance at life for Taylor Grant? Bending down, he placed a light kiss on her cheek.

"Good night, princess. See you in the morning."

For the rest of the evening the phone rang incessantly until finally, in frustration, Taylor took it off the hook. The reporters would not let up. Had they been calling this relentlessly since his article came out? Grimly, he paced the length of the silent living room, ruthlessly examining his own behavior, but refusing to look too closely at his personal feelings for Katie. Sitting at the Queen Anne desk in the corner, he tried to make sense out of his notes. At eleven, Taylor decided to go to bed.

Finding a blanket and pillow in the bedroom closet, he left the door ajar—in case Katie woke up feeling disoriented, and needed him. He remembered how she'd insisted he take the bed—and smiled. She'd been too exhausted to think of that tonight, no doubt. As he made his bed on the small bamboo settee, he had a vivid image of how beautiful she had looked asleep in the bathtub. Having knocked several times, he'd gotten worried. He'd opened the door. The sight of Katie, dark hair piled atop her head and curled by the steam, had sent an ache of longing through him. Her flesh was pink from the hot water, and she looked incredibly tranquil. Her body was firm and supple, breasts small but nicely formed. He had brushed such thoughts away and, concerned, had lifted her out of the water and into his arms. Her flesh was slippery and yielding beneath his grip as she collapsed against him, fighting to awaken . . .

Taking a deep breath now, Taylor undressed in the bathroom. He showered quickly and slipped into blue drawstring pajama bottoms. He wore no top, and his broad chest caught the moonlight as he walked softly into Katie's bedroom. A feeling of great yearning passed over him. Lord, how he wanted to lie down and gather Katie's small form against him. Just to sleep with her in his arms . . . Taylor banished the idea, berating himself as he walked quietly back out into the living room. He wanted Katie— all of her. Body and soul and mind. And he knew this was no light matter. She couldn't ever be a one-night stand. Would never allow herself to be. She was a woman who needed a permanent and lasting relationship . . . Grimacing, he lowered himself onto the small settee, letting it creak in protest under his two-hundred-some-odd pounds.

"Tough," he muttered to the piece of furniture, "you're just going to have to take it on the chin."

He drew the sheet to his waist and punched the pillow into a softer form that was more comfortable. A wry smile lingered on his lips. Right now he could be in that room with Katie in his arms. He knew she would come to him. He had seen the longing in her gaze. He closed his eyes. Give her time, Taylor. Time. She's a butterfly, and until you're able to offer her something more . . . Yet he was hungry for the feel, the touch, the fragrance, the sight of her. He was happiest when he was near her. Mentally he reran the day's events. Katie . . . Katie . . . Lord, she was so exquisitely vulnerable . . . and then sleep stole the last of his lingering thoughts. Thoughts that blazed with emotion he ached to share with only her. And he knew Katie would treat his feelings with the greatest of care. Treasure . . . she was a salve to his badly scarred heart, and he longed to possess her body and soul . . . forever.

Chapter 8

DARK, MARAUDING SHAPES stained her ordinarily brilliant dreams. Katie tossed and turned in her bed, the pale blue sheet twisted beneath her. Her heart picked up a dreaded beat, panic licking through every nerve in her body. She watched in terror as a large, shadowy shape congealed into the form of a man. An arm was raised and a rock hurled through the front window of her bookstore. Glass shattered and splintered like a shimmer of rainbow fragments and Katie screamed, retreating to the back of the store. Her panic turned to hysteria as she saw a bottle with a flaming rag in the top. The bottle exploded into a wall of flame as it skidded across the purple carpet of the bookshop. And then, as she crouched, arms thrown across her face, she cried out for help.

"Katie? Katie, wake up!"

She moaned, caught in the throes of the nightmare. The

sinister shape of the man walking through the flames, grinning at her. Coming for her . . . Trying to wrench free of the hand that held her shoulder, Katie jerked awake.

"Katie? Easy, take it easy."

A sob tore from her throat as she looked up . . . up into Taylor's shadowed face. With a strangled sound she realized, finally, that this wasn't her assailant. Taylor! It was Taylor. She threw her arms around him, burying her head beneath his jaw.

"Taylor," she said, her voice muffled.

Worried, he held her, rocked her in his arms. She was trembling. "Just a bad dream, princess," he soothed, kissing her tangled hair. "Nothing more. You're all right. You're safe."

She allowed his voice to drive away the terror coursing through her, the vision of the grinning arsonist slowly dissolving. Only when Taylor eased her away and began drying her cheeks did Katie realize she was crying.

"I-I'm sorry," she gulped and looked over at the nightstand. The clock told her it was two in the morning.

"Shh, nothing to apologize for." Taylor studied her with a frightening intensity. Katie's eyes were wide with shock, her pupils huge and black. In the moonlight, her skin looked taut and pale. "That was some dream!"

Katie wrapped her arms protectively around herself. "I usually have such lovely dreams, Taylor. Sometimes there's tension, but—never nightmares like this," she quavered. "It was so real . . ."

He caressed her hair, wanting to soothe her. "Tell me about it."

"I dreamed I was in my bookstore. A rock came through the window. Next came a bottle with a flaming rag. I ran to the back of the store as it exploded into flames." She took in an unsteady breath, risking a glance at him. "It was the man who calls me on the phone, Taylor. He came through a wall of flames to get me. He had an evil smile. Oh,

Taylor. Am I losing my mind?"

Taking her into his arms, Taylor held her tightly. "Listen to me, princess. The last couple of days have put one hell of a strain on you. That nightmare was nothing more than a reflection of your fear."

Stubbornly, Katie shook her head, needing Taylor's warmth. "No."

"What?"

She shut her eyes tightly. "Sometimes I get premonitions," she blurted. "I had one the night before my parents died. I called and told them not to come." Her voice grew bleak. "They didn't listen . . ."

With an effort, Taylor kept his thoughts to himself. Katie was worn out. She needed time away from all this, time in which to pull herself together. He pushed her gently toward the center of the bed. "Okay, princess. Move over."

Katie was too shaken to realize what Taylor was doing until he slipped into her bed beside her. He pulled her into his arms.

"Now," he told her, his voice low and husky, "I want you to close your eyes and go back to sleep. You won't have any more nightmares, Katie. I'll keep them away."

Battered by the emotions slowly ebbing within her, Katie acquiesced. She turned to Taylor, her head resting in the hollow of his shoulder, her small hand caught in the dark mat of hair on his chest. He was her knight. He would protect her. Gratitude overwhelmed her, and she closed her eyes.

"I'm so tired," she whispered, her words slurred with exhaustion.

"I know you are, Katie. Sleep . . . I'll be here if you need me. I promise."

Taylor lay awake for a long time. Katie's first scream had pulled him bolt upright on the creaky settee. Her second scream had sent him stumbling through the living room. He had thought she was being attacked by an intruder. He stared up at the gauzy drapes suspended over the bed; the moonlight cast a muted radiance about the room. He found Katie wrapped in a tangle of sheets, her face frozen in fear. It was then he realized she was only having a nightmare.

Disturbed now by her nearness, Taylor tried to concentrate on anything but her pliant form pressed against him. Her breasts were soft and so was her breathing. She was fast asleep, thank the Lord. Absently, he caressed her shoulder, savoring the feel of the silk robe against her flesh. The lilac scent that was so much a part of Katie surrounded him, and an ache grew in his lower body. Shutting his eyes tightly, Taylor fought back his burgeoning need. He should have tucked her in and gone back to the living room. But his need for her was too strong; he couldn't make himself leave her. Taylor Grant, he thought bitterly, was always in control of everything in his life. Including his sex drive—which had now, inexplicably, gone out of control. Not to mention his heart . . .

Katie. It was Katie's fault. She was a witch. No, it was his own fault. For opening himself to her—for responding to her honesty, her delicious warmth . . . Taylor wrestled with himself for nearly an hour, trying to forget Katie was nestled in the crook of his arm, that she trusted him. Hell, she'd be better off in a cage with a hungry tiger. It was only with supreme effort that Taylor finally placed a check on his starving need to make love to the woman who slept softly against him . . .

Now, instead, he searched his mind for ways to ease the pressures that were closing in on her, disturbing her sleep. He ran their conversations back through his mind, gathering the facts. Finally, at four in the morning, he had settled on a plan. Satisfied, Taylor's lids drooped, and he turned on his side, drawing his princess deep into his embrace and sleeping soundly for the first time in days.

*   *   *

Katie was awakened by the muted sound of someone whistling. She wrinkled her nose, stretched, and felt the sunlight pouring through the windows behind her bed. Happiness, emanating from some unknown source, surged through her as she opened her eyes to drink in the radiance of the sun. And then her expression clouded with memories of the night before. Her premonition . . . and then Taylor had come in and held her . . .

Katie sat up quickly, her hair in a tangled disarray around her face. Taylor had slept in her bed last night! A whirl of desparate emotions danced through her, and she tried to assimilate them all.

"Good morning."

Pleasure reverberated through Katie as she looked up. Taylor leaned casually against the open door, and he took her breath away. He was clean-shaven, his gray eyes clear with an unspoken warmth, and a smile lingered on his well-shaped mouth. A quiver of desire darted through her. Had something happened last night—something she couldn't recall? Was that why he seemed so intimate this morning? She lifted her fingers to her brow, trying to will her memory of last night back into her drowsy mind.

Taylor straightened, frowning. "Do you have a head-ache, Katie?"

"No . . ." She managed a feeble smile. "I was just trying to remember what happened last night."

Her cheeks flushed. "Nothing to worry about," he reassured her.

The tub! Katie's eyes widened. "I fell asleep in the tub last night!"

Taylor tried very hard not to smile and almost succeeded. "Yeah, you did."

With a groan, Katie covered her face. "I always fall asleep in there! I forgot to warn you about that."

He crossed his arms. "Well, after forty-five minutes I got worried, Katie. Sorry . . ." Liar! he thought. He wasn't sorry at all. "Wasn't much to it," he went on in a business-like fashion, "I just dried you off, put you in your robe, and carried you to bed." And then his voice grew gentler. "You were exhausted last night. You only woke up once. You had a bad dream, sweetheart. I came in to see that you were all right. That was all."

She raised her eyes, utterly mortified, but had the good grace to accept his explanation. "You won't put that in your exclusive, will you?"

Soberly, Taylor shook his head. He sauntered up to her, the desire to sift his fingers through that ebony hair excruciating. Katie looked drowsy, inviting, and so much a woman, wrapped in her silk robe! "What we do in our personal life is none of anyone's business," he promised somberly.

"Spoken like a true Scorpio." Suddenly, Katie was glad he was born under that sign. "Scorpios value privacy above all else."

Taylor smiled down at her. "I think Sagittarians must, too." He reached out to brush his knuckles lightly against her flaming cheek.

Katie closed her eyes, overwhelmed. "I owe you," she said, meeting his dove-gray gaze. "I remember that nightmare. And how you held me afterward . . . Thank you."

Taylor hunched down, his hand resting on the edge of the mattress. "I'm glad it happened, Katie. It showed me something."

"What?"

"How tired you are. How much you need a rest."

Her blue eyes glimmered with tenderness. "I thought you were going to make fun of me."

"Never. Anyway, once you're up and dressed, we'll take the day off. I called Maud and she agreed to watch the store today so that I can steal you away and let you recuperate." He smiled recklessly. He had her, for once! "And I've managed to put together a picnic basket, found a blanket, and all I need is you. What do you say?"

Katie sat open-mouthed for a moment. "Why—I think it's a wonderful idea!"

He stood, shoving his hands into the pockets of his beige chino pants. "I knew you'd see it my way," he said, obviously pleased with himself.

With a laugh of delight, Katie threw off the covers. The robe had loosened during the night . . . Blushing, she hastily retied the belt, got up, and threw her arms around Taylor's neck.

"Thank you, Taylor," she whispered.

Unprepared for her enthusiasm, Taylor took a step back. But he recovered quickly, and a ribbon of happiness flowed through him. Embracing Katie, he pressed a kiss to her temple. "You're welcome, princess." And then, reluctantly, he released her, wondering what it would be like to wake up every morning with Katie at his side . . .

Taylor excused himself and ambled back to the kitchen to finish packing the basket. When he had awakened this morning, it was with an overwhelming sense of happiness. The feeling was foreign to him; he'd never felt that way with Mary Ann. Was it Katie's crazy Arabian Nights bedroom decor that did it? The birds singing right outside the window? The sun turning the room into a muted pastel fantasy? What? The more time he spent around Katie, the more his logic—which had always served him so faithfully!—deserted him. More and more he was relying on his emotions, paying closer attention to them than he ever had before. He packed the last of their meal, closed the wicker basket, and sighed deeply. It was Katie, and that irrepressible spirit of hers. She *was* a sorceress, weaving her spell, robbing him of the ability to think . . . teaching him to feel.

Shaking his head, Taylor picked up the basket and walked into the living room to wait for Katie. The phone was still off the hook; earlier in the morning he had replaced the receiver only to take five calls in a row, all from reporters. Maybe he should put it back again. Grimacing, Taylor thought about how the journalists would continue to hound Katie. He wasn't proud of his colleagues at this moment . . .

"Taylor?"

He started at the sound of Katie's voice, then turned. His heart pounded at the sight of her. She was dressed in a body-fitting lime-green top and a bright yellow skirt that almost touched her ankles. On her feet were delicate white sandals. She looked like lemon and lime: refreshing, beautiful. Her hair was tied in a knot with yellow ribbon, a few tendrils escaping to frame her expressive face.

"Yes?" His voice was low.

She smiled. "Have you chosen a spot for our picnic?"

"Maud said you had a favorite glen up in the hills. Your . . . magic place?"

Katie's smile broadened. "Wonderful! I'm glad I wore my swim suit," she said, pointing to the lime-green top. Do you have one?"

He shook his head. "Maud didn't mention swimming."

Picking up a small, rainbow-colored canvas bag, she joined him. "Let's stop at your place and get you some swim trunks, then."

Taylor nodded and escorted her out of the apartment. Inwardly, he winced. He didn't want Katie to see where he lived—not after he'd experienced her place. She had created a home. He lived in a silent skeleton of a house. When they arrived at the small pink stucco one-story on the outskirts of Rio Conchos, Taylor grew tense. Katie insisted on going in with him while he retrieved the swim trunks.

The look on her face told him everything. She stood in the center of the living room, stricken.

"Taylor, you haven't even begun to unpack!"

"I haven't had time," he said, and disappeared into the bedroom.

Katie looked around. All the blinds were drawn, leaving the room dark. Just like a Scorpio's nest, she decided. The house was nearly empty and the highly polished wood floors were in serious need of dusting. Not wanting to hurt his feelings, she resolved to say nothing more about his house. The fact that he refused to meet her eyes told her much; he was uncomfortable about allowing her into his private world. Typical Scorpio, she decided. Well, she'd fix him! A plan began to form in her mind . . .

It was a lovely day. Taylor guided the car effortlessly through the California hills, now covered with verdant grass. The rains had been kind this year. By mid-May, the lack of water would turn these hills yellow, and they would remain so until December or January. At last Katie pointed to a small dirt road that passed between two rolling hills. Carefully he drove up through the winding lane that took them deeper into an isolated area, devoid of homes or people.

"There!" she said excitedly, pointing to his left. "Can you see the glen?"

Taylor's spirits rose at the lilt of her voice. Her enthusiasm was contagious, and right now he needed a lift: He still felt embarrassed that Katie had seen his house. Ahead he could see where the road ended at the base of the hill. There was a small lake, shaped like an oval and shaded by scrub oak. Braking the car to a halt at the crest of the hill, Taylor was stunned: The hills that surrounded the glen were carpeted with millions of golden California poppies and wind poppies. The breeze moved through them like an invisible hand, causing golden and scarlet heads to bow briefly.

"Isn't it beautiful?" Katie breathed, taking in the panorama of unrelenting color.

Taylor could find no words; he was deluged with feeling. "I've never seen anything like this," he admitted finally, easing the Trans Am down the hill.

"You're used to steel, glass, and concrete, right?"

He grinned. "I'm a city boy, Katie. Does it show?"

"I think you have a country soul."

"Uh-oh, is it catching?"

Her laughter filled the car. "And what if it was, Taylor Grant? What's wrong with being touched by beauty? Of flowers, a shimmering blue lake, the green of oak trees?"

Nothing, he thought, an ache filling him. Taylor stopped the car beneath a stand of oak and got out. He was seeing yet another facet of this compelling woman, he realized: Katie in the out-of-doors. The hills vibrated with the golds and reds. A pair of noisy blue jays added to the sound of bees humming and the sigh of a whispery breeze.

The sun had reached its zenith by the time they spread the black-and-white checkered blanket beneath a towering oak. Taylor watched in amazement as Katie bloomed before his eyes; it was as if she were taking sustenance from the glen. But wasn't he, too? He felt the tension drain from him as he lay on his side and sipped at a plastic cup of tart rosé wine.

"I think you like my glen," Katie teased, coming to sit by him, her yellow skirt looking very feminine as it swirled about her slender legs.

"I do feel relaxed. But I think it's the wine."

Katie grinned. "Why can't you accept that it's the energy here?"

Taylor reached over, caressing her bare arm, aware of her softness and, ensuingly, of his need for her. "No, it's you," he told her seriously. And then he glanced around at the poppies. "The rest is only window dressing, princess."

Sobering, Katie met his deep gray eyes. She saw that his mouth no longer drew in at the corners and that the perpetual V no longer hovered between his brows. Taylor *was* relaxed. Impulsively she picked a poppy and held it gently in her hands.

"Did you know that Victorian ladies used poppies to test the affections of their lovers?"

He smiled. "How?"

"A woman would place a petal in the palm of one hand and then clap her hands together. If there was a loud slap, it meant her man still loved her. If there was no sound, then she knew he loved someone else."

"And at this time of year, I suppose every woman in California comes up here to find a poppy and test her man?"

Katie plucked the petals from her poppy and showered him with them; golden rain, falling softly. "I doubt it." She shrugged, still as enthralled by the beauty that surrounded them as she'd been the moment they arrived. She took a deep breath and closed her eyes. "All flowers, plants, and trees have stories—we have only to listen," she whispered.

"And you know most of those stories, don't you?" She'd make such a wonderful mother, Taylor thought for the second time in as many days. And for a shattering split second, he dreamed that she carried his child. The fantasy left him feeling naked and vulnerable. Yet as he studied Katie's profile, the fantasy seemed to grow in strength, until he could scarcely bear the welter of feeling roused in him.

"Some, not all," she corrected, getting to her feet. She held out her hand. "Come, let's take a walk first before we eat."

He took her small hand, allowing himself to be swayed by her eagerness, and accepted that today was a gift. Tomorrow reality would once again claim them, but he wouldn't let it intrude now. No, he resolved to allow Katie's joy to infect him, lift him above the quagmire of his daily life . . .

She pointed out other plants or flowers as they walked. Near the stream that wound through the hills on its way to the lake below were patches of blue lupine, their blue-violet flowers waving on slender stalks. There were also cream cups, which looked exactly like their name. And then Katie pointed out the scarlet columbine.

Taylor leaned down, plucking one of these exquisite scarlet flowers. "Here," he said, and placed the flower behind her ear. "Now you look like Persephone."

Katie's eyes lit with amusement. "Persephone? The Greek goddess who was kidnapped by dark, brooding Pluto?"

He grinned and suddenly swept her into his arms. "Today, I'm Pluto. I'm going to kidnap you, and . . ." He didn't finish the sentiment.

She threw her arms around his neck, laughing. "Just as long as you don't take me underground, I'll come willingly."

"Come to my blanket," he teased.

"Okay."

"And I'll share my food with you."

"Okay."

She was feather-light in his arms, and he breathed deeply of her lilac scent. "Why aren't you putting up a fight? Some Persephone you are!"

"Because I'm starved!"

Laughing, Taylor eased Katie to the ground and onto the blanket. Before he knew what was happening, she had placed a quick kiss on his mouth. The kiss of a butterfly. His lips tingled in the aftermath of this spontaneous show of affection. Seeming not to notice, Katie quickly divided the fare between them, then sat down next to him.

"I couldn't find any meat in your refrigerator," Taylor noted unhappily, looking down at the peanut butter sandwiches.

"I don't eat meat."

"You and my photographer," he muttered.

She smiled, munching contentedly on the sandwich. "This has as much protein as meat."

"Don't you start on me, too."

"Was I picking on you?"

"Yes, and you know it. I can see that gleam in your eye."

Katie feigned surprise. "A Scorpio never misses a thing," she teased.

He lay back, propping himself up with one arm as he polished off another sandwich, then began on a crisp red apple. "I'm a reporter. I'm trained not to miss much."

"I think you'd be good at any work that requires detail. Did you always want to be a reporter, Taylor?"

Taylor shrugged. "As a kid, I wanted to be a cop. Is that a good Scorpio occupation?"

She smiled. "Very much so. So is a detective."

"When I went to college I got interested in journalism. I suppose it was because I saw what influence the press could have." He frowned down at the half-eaten apple. "I graduated with honors and a whole lot of idealistic theories about how, as a reporter, I could make the world a better place to live."

Katie heard the disillusionment in his voice. "What happened to make you alter that view, Taylor?"

"Getting a job as a crime reporter. I wanted to do exposés, and that's what I did. I didn't realize quite how badly it was getting to me—the sort of people I was dealing with, the destroyed lives. And then, last year, I got a new editor. I did one gut-wrenching series on the street people in New York. I spent months among them. It nearly tore me apart." He set the apple aside, staring at the calm surface of the lake. "And after I'd busted my tail on that assignment and put myself through an emotional wringer, the editor wouldn't run the piece."

Katie frowned. "Why?"

"It wasn't flashy enough. He wanted me to concentrate on the teenage hookers. Sex sells papers, he said. He wasn't interested in the total story."

Katie shook her head. "That isn't good journalism!"

"That's what I told him. We got into one hell of a fight." Taylor snorted softly. "Actually, I should thank the jerk. It was the final straw in a life that was already going bad. Ultimately it was what made me quit my job and move to California."

Katie reached out, her fingertips resting lightly on his arm. "You were very tired, weren't you?"

His flesh tingled beneath her touch. Lord, did Katie know how she affected him? Clearly she didn't. One look into those caring eyes, and he knew she would never tease him.

"Tired? I was burned out. I destroyed my marriage. I blew my job. Yeah, when I left New York, there was no going back. Everything had changed for me there. What I had was gone—"

"You blame yourself for the failure of your marriage. Why?"

He gazed up at her. "How many relationships have you had, Katie?"

"Enough. You see me as a scatterbrained idealist—and I admit that I've made my share of mistakes in life. On the human level, I mean."

"Sometimes I can't believe you've been with a man," he admitted quietly. "You seem so innocent... You're so different from most women."

"Not so different, believe me," she assured him. "Without going into my own sordid past, let me say that I know what it takes to make a relationship grow or die, Taylor. And I can't understand why you take all the blame for what happened to your marriage. Marriage is never a one-way street."

"It was for me."

"Did you love Mary Ann?"

He nodded. "When I married her, I thought it would be

forever. I made a commitment to her that I'd never made to another woman. And she was incredibly beautiful."

Katie gauged the pain in his voice. "Beauty that was skin deep, or beauty from the heart?" she posed.

"You're right. You're not as naive as I thought." But the halfhearted attempt at a smile died on his lips. "No, Mary Ann didn't have beauty from the heart. In the beginning, I thought she did."

"When did you marry her?"

"Right after I began to get some recognition. I'd won a number of prestigious journalism awards within a short time. I was on the Manhattan party circuit—a newcomer, and a little uncomfortable with it, but there. Anyway, I was at one of the swankier affairs—it looked like a Who's Who of New York City. Mary Ann was there. She hadn't been in the city long—she was from a small midwestern town and had signed with one of the smaller modeling agencies. I was talking to the owner of the biggest agency in town. Mary Ann came up and introduced herself. One thing led to another as we stood there talking, and Mary Ann got an appointment to see the agency head the following day. The rest is history: We got married after a whirlwind courtship, and her career shot up like a meteor."

Katie bit her lip and nodded. Mary Ann had been a user, she guessed. She had ridden on the coattails of Taylor's hard-earned success and had used his connections to launch her own career. "And as her career blossomed, you began to grow apart?" Katie queried.

"Yeah. She had a lot of overseas modeling assignments. And when she was in New York, she liked to party. Of course, I was on the night beat and couldn't always join her. There wasn't much room for compromise."

Katie's heart ached for him. Even now, Taylor didn't realize he'd been used. Or perhaps he knew and didn't want to admit it. Maybe the realization was just too painful. Katie couldn't blame him if that was the case.

Katie looked at him somberly. "All right. Let's talk about—"

"No more about me. I've exposed enough for one day, Katie Riordan."

He was teasing her again, and she responded. "As if I'm going to go tell all of Rio Conchos about you."

"I know you keep plenty of secrets. And I wouldn't have told out anything if I didn't trust you."

Katie chuckled. "Scorpios trust so rarely. But when they do, it's completely." She lifted her cup. "Here's a toast to our mutual trust."

Taylor raised his cup, feeling guilty. "I betrayed your trust the first day I met you, Katie. Why are you giving me a second chance? I know I wouldn't be so generous."

She laughed. "Sagittarians are different. We're generally forgiving. Maybe because we know we're fallible. So we don't consider it the end of the world when other people make mistakes. Like Scorpios do."

His smile warmed his eyes as he watched her. "Is there anything *good* about being a Scorpio?"

"Of course there is!"

"What?"

"They're quiet, passionate, proud—and very loyal. Once a Scorpio loves you, it's forever. I like Scorpios. My mother was one. Maud is, too." Katie's eyes twinkled. "And now you. I'm surrounded by a sea of scorpions."

He cocked his head. "And the scorpion's sting can be lethal. Aren't you afraid we'll do you in?"

With a delighted laugh, Katie got to her feet. She unbuttoned her skirt, allowing it to fall to her feet, and slipped off her sandals. "You Scorpios think you're so big and bad. Come on, I'm ready for a swim. How about you?"

She was a sunbeam, Taylor decided, stripping down to the black swimming trunks he'd donned at his house. Well, sunbeams never stayed still for long. Katie had grabbed her brightly colored beach towel and was running toward the lake. Spreading the rainbow-hued towel over the lush grass, she tugged off her hair ribbon, releasing a cascade of black curls. She gave Taylor an impatient look and walked gingerly to the water's edge, calling for him to hurry.

As he laid his olive-drab towel next to hers, Taylor shook his head. If he hadn't know Katie was a healer, that she ran a crazy bookstore filled with odd tomes, he would think she was just your everyday beautiful woman at this moment. Her bathing suit clung lovingly to her body, and she played in the water like a seal pup. His grin widened as he waded in after her.

During the next half-hour, Taylor learned to play. When Katie dived and grabbed him by the feet, pulling him under water, he was unprepared. He fought his way to the surface, spitting and gasping for air. Katie swam out a good distance. Then she stopped, treading water and laughing.

Taylor wiped the water from his eyes and stalked her. He certainly planned to even the score! Physical activity hadn't been one of his avocations back in New York. He hadn't swum in years. Consequently Katie was able to elude him quite effectively at first. Finally he caught her on the other side of the small lake. Hands spanning her small waist, he lifted her from the water until her smiling eyes were level with his own.

"I ought to dunk you," he gasped.

Katie grinned, her fingers gripping his hard, muscular shoulders. Hair clung to her face, and she blinked away the water. "Well, go ahead. Get even with me. Scorpios love revenge."

Gray eyes smoldered with fire as he drew her to him. "I extract my revenge this way," he said.

Katie was unprepared. Her breath caught in her throat as his mouth captured hers. He was warm and strong and tasted of tart apple. A quiver sang through her body as he molded her to him; the water was cool, his flesh hot. With a sigh, she settled her arms on his shoulders, feeling the heavy beat of his heart. And as she felt his maleness harden against her, fire leaped crazily through her. Each nip of his mouth made her dizzy with need.

"Taylor," she whispered, her breath ragged against his mouth, "I want you . . . so badly. . ."

His hands followed the contours of her body, sliding down over her bottom, pinning her against him, letting her know just how much he hungered for her, too. He was aware of her nipples against his chest, the flutter of her heart. There was nothing fragile about Katie now. She was all woman, responding to him like a woman, and driving him to the edge of reason. Taylor knew if he didn't stop, she would carry him over that barrier of no return. He had great self-control; but once it was breached, he couldn't go back . . .

With a groan, he gently eased Katie away. He saw the disappointment shadowed in her eyes, and felt bad. Words —the deeply personal words that came so hard to him— were not there to explain why he had broken the intimacy that simmered between them.

"Come on," he said thickly, releasing her. "Let's lie on the bank and get some sun. I'm cold." Liar. He throbbed with a fiery heat, and he ached to make love to her. The hurt in her eyes made him feel even worse as he took her hand and helped her from the water. He dropped an arm across her shoulders and steered her around the lake toward their towels.

Her skin still glistened with water and after she plopped down on her belly, Taylor took his towel and dried her off. She smiled, head resting on her arms.

"You know, I didn't realize how long your hair is," he murmured, running several strands through his fingers. Damp silk, he thought as he allowed the strands to fall back across her shoulder.

"It's about halfway down to my waist," she said, closing her eyes. Taylor's touch made her feel like a cherished gift, and she almost forgot the earlier hurt of his withdrawal. "But it's so curly that when it's dry, it looks much shorter than it really is."

He spread his damp towel and eased himself down on it. Mere inches separated them; the sun felt good on his skin. "I like your hair," he said. "When I first saw you, I was sure you were a Gypsy fortune teller."

Katie chuckled. "You weren't far from wrong."

"You don't tell fortunes. You heal with your hands."

She opened her eyes, met his, and in that instant, knew he was serious. "You've finally accepted that I can heal?"

"You sound skeptical."

She smiled. "I am. What changed your mind?"

"You."

"What do you mean, Taylor?" Her heart beat harder, and she realized that his answer was very important to her. Something miraculous was taking place between them, and she couldn't quite believe it. Taylor had been so suspicious of her. Hadn't he all but called her a fake in his article? Now he looked almost boyish, damp hair grazing his brow, the harsh lines gone from his face.

"It's you, Katie. I can't explain it. I see you differently now. Hell, I can't explain it, I can only feel it. Spending these last few days with you has changed my mind."

A feeling of warmth flowed through Katie, and she savored it. "So, now that you believe in me—do I become a specimen to be studied?"

Taylor blinked. "A specimen?"

"Yes."

"Hell no!"

"Don't take offense."

"I do."

"I know. I'm sorry."

He relaxed slightly, wanting to cup her delicate face and

kiss her. And she must have read the intention in his eyes, because she propped herself up, leaned over, and placed her lips directly on his. She was sweet, her breath moist across his cheek, and he groaned.

"Katie, no . . ." he said thickly.

She broke contact, studying him from beneath her lashes. "Why not, Taylor?"

He shook his head. "Look," he said hoarsely, "I try to maintain semblance of control, princess, but you're making it pretty darned hard."

"But I want you."

Shaken by her honesty, Taylor reached up, caressing her cheek. "Katie—"

"Is it that you don't want me? Is it because you see me as . . . as different, Taylor?"

He heard the pain in her voice; he saw it in her eyes. Cursing, he sat up. He took her hands in his. "It has absolutely nothing to do with that, sweetheart. Absolutely nothing." And suddenly he remembered that Katie had told him her fiancé had dropped her for that very reason. "Is that what you think? That I see you as a freak of some kind and therefore don't want you?"

Katie nodded and turned away from him.

"No!" he hissed. "Katie, you're the most desirable woman I've ever met. And more than anything else, I want you. Do you hear me? I've never ached like this for a woman. You tie me in knots. Every time you look at me with those huge, soulful eyes of yours, I go nuts."

She turned her head to meet his thunderous eyes. "Then why do you push me away? Can a kiss shared be so wrong?"

Taylor took an unsteady breath. "Listen to me," he began. "When I kiss you I want to go far beyond that, Katie. I don't have any control when it comes to you." He looked toward the lake. "And dammit, you're not the sort of woman who has casual relationships. I could never hurt you, Katie. I would never want to. And I'm just not sure—"

He wanted to tell her that if he made love to her, she would—and should—expect a commitment from him. A lasting one. And right now, he was still too haunted by his past, by his divorce; he couldn't think clearly. He couldn't let himself hurt Katie just because he was tied up in knots. She deserved a hell of a lot better than that. And before anything happened between them, he wanted to be sure he could give it.

"Look," he went on, "I've hurt you once already. Deeply. I never expected to grow so close to you, Katie. Or—" The word *love* nearly escaped his lips, and this shocked him. "I'm still suffering over my divorce, Katie. I'm still reeling from all the changes I've been through. And I won't drag you through them with me. As much as I want to—and as much as I want you right now. But I'll be damned if I'll add to your problems. You've got enough already. Some of which I *have* caused. I'll never forgive myself for that article, dammit. And now, in addition to the reporters hounding you, you've got some nut threatening your life. You don't need me to contribute any more problems than those I've already inflicted."

She tried to smile. "Thanks, Taylor," she said, squeezing his hands.

"Thanks for what?" he growled.

"For being honest with me and for being yourself." I love you for that, Katie added silently. And she did. There as no rhyme or reason for the feelings in her heart; she only knew that Taylor was special as no other man had been before. Where would all of this lead? He had been wounded by his divorce. He had hurt her in another way. Taylor saw only his failings; he knew little of what was good about himself. Katie smiled and leaned over to place a chaste kiss on his cheek.

"This evening?"

"Yes?" he said, puzzled.

"Will you help me make dinner?"

Taylor groaned and flopped back down on the towel, throwing an arm across his eyes. "Katie, I'm the world's worst cook. I burn water."

"If you insist on living with me till we catch my threatening caller, you're going to have to pull your own weight, Taylor Grant. That means cooking, too." Somehow, Katie would begin to show him that he wasn't such a bad person after all. She planned to do it through little things. For Katie, it was the small, thoughtful gestures that counted the most between people. Her eyes grew tender as she stared down at Taylor. The cosmos worked in strange and unexpected ways, she thought. And she was glad.

Chapter 9

THE PHONE WAS ringing when Katie opened the door. Her smile disappeared as Taylor walked over to answer it.

"Probably just another damn reporter harassing you," he said. The afterglow from their beautiful day together shattered around her, and Katie barely nodded, locking the door behind her. She purposely blocked out the call and went to the bathroom to shower and change.

Taylor was grim when she reappeared, dressed in a pale pink sundress.

"What's wrong?" she asked.

"I've got to go, Katie. That was a call from my office. There's been a hazardous-materials spill twenty miles from here, and Dean Gerus, the editor-in-chief, wants Barry and me to cover it. The spill is pretty big, and the stuff is poisonous as hell. Lives could be lost. It's a big story. It's my job, Katie. I can't turn it down." Taylor ran his fingers through his hair and walked over to her. She was smiling up at him. His frown disappeared as he drank her in. He settled his hands on her small shoulders. "You're like a butterfly; every time you change, it's into something prettier and more colorful."

Katie continued to smile, but it took all her effort. "Thank you. Taylor . . . be careful. My intuition tells me you're right—this is dangerous." Her eyes turned dark with pleading, and she slipped her arms around him. "Promise?"

Sighing and thinking that this woman was all he wanted for the rest of his life, Taylor rested his head against her freshly washed hair. "For you, I'll be careful."

A shiver of longing coursed through Katie, and she lifted her head. She was not to be disappointed. His mouth moved gently across hers, and for one magical moment she lost herself in his fiery, tender touch. She had stolen a moment from reality, here in his arms. She wanted nothing more. Ever.

Taylor eased Katie from his arms and caressed the curling ends of her hair lightly. "Sorry I won't be able to help you cook dinner, princess."

"You wouldn't have wanted it anyway. We were going to make tofu surprise."

He grinned. "Tofu surprise? You're right. I don't even know what tofu is."

Earlier in the day Taylor had checked all the locks on the windows, so he knew they were secure. Katie was in the kitchen, whipping up tofu surprise. Actually, the smell issuing from that room wasn't so bad, Taylor conceded, as he threw a lightweight linen sports jacket over one shoulder. His mouth watered. He was hungry. One look at Katie in a bright red checked apron that stood out gaily against the pink sundress, and he was a man starved. He wanted to tell her that the colors she wore would be gaudy and mismatched on anyone else. And then he smiled because Katie's naturalness far outshone anything she wore or didn't wear . . .

"I'm going, Katie. Make sure you lock the door after me. And don't answer it. If the reporters start hounding you again, take the phone off the hook."

"I'll be okay, Taylor." She quickly tossed snow peas, water chestnuts, and a handful of cashews into the wok, preparing to stir-fry them. "You're the one who has to be careful. Do you have the key?"

Taylor held it up. "Right here. I'll be back as soon as I can, Katie. Don't worry about me."

Don't worry about him, Katie fumed, gnawing on her lower lip. She had slipped into a white cotton nightgown that brushed her ankles. The clock read midnight. He had been gone seven hours already. She went to the closet and retrieved the sheets and blankets. She knew very little about hazardous-material spills, only that they were dangerous. Was Taylor being careful? Would he take foolish risks to get his story?

She fluffed the pillow and placed it at one end of the settee, snuggling beneath the sheet and lightweight blanket. Tonight Taylor could have the bed. He was simply too long for this little couch. True to Taylor's prediction, the phone had begun to ring with reporters' queries shortly after he left, and the receiver now lay beside it on the table. As much as she wanted to put it back—she felt very cut off this way—she knew it wasn't wise. She had called Maud earlier and learned that several reporters had been to the bookstore during the day, looking for Katie.

"I told them you went to San Diego," Maud had chortled in pleased tones. "At least I got rid of 'em for you temporarily."

A smile played on Katie's lips as she closed her eyes, thinking of Maud's warm countenance. Without her friends and Taylor, she would have been defenseless. Hugging the pillow in her arms, Katie sighed and slipped into a deep sleep, her dreams brilliant, colorful, and pleasant because Taylor was in them.

At three in the morning, the parking lot behind Katie's building was empty. The lights of the Trans Am stabbed through the darkness as Taylor made the final turn into the lot. Out of long habit, he let his gaze sweep the shadowy recesses of the poorly lit brick structure. He froze. And then blinked once to make sure he wasn't seeing things. There! He slammed on the brakes as he saw a man's figure dart from the doorway of Katie's bookstore. Taylor jerked the car door open and leaped out.

"Hey!" he thundered and then took off in pursuit.

The sound of metal grating against metal broke the dark silence of the early morning hour. Katie moved slightly, but did not awaken. In her dreams she watched the brass doorknob move slowly to the left. The distinct click of the latch followed. Light slitted through the opening as the door moved, and the shadowy form of a man slipped silently through.

Taylor rubbed his smarting eyes as he shut the door quietly and locked it behind him. He was still breathing hard. His shirt clung damply to his chest and back. Dammit, he hadn't caught the intruder.

Was this Katie's anonymous caller? Or was it someone else, drawn to Katie due to all the damn publicity Taylor had caused? Agitated, he stood for a few moments, staring through the junglelike living room. In the pale glow of a single lamp, he saw that Katie was fast asleep on the settee. A warmth spread through him, easing his tension. At last a tired smile creased his face as he moved over to where she slept. There was a hand-scribbled note on the coffee table, and he leaned down to retrieve it.

"Take the bed, Taylor. You're too short for this settee

and it's just right for me. Wake me when you get home. Katie."

Exhaustion lapped at him as he studied the note and then her serene face. Home. Lord, how good that sounded! It was almost as if . . . as if they were married. The thought lingered in Taylor's mind. Katie's blanket had slipped off, and he bent to pull it over her again. He was sweaty and dirty, and all he wanted was a hot shower and sleep. The note notwithstanding, he didn't want to wake her. He kissed her cheek instead and got up, moving through the apartment, which smelled of the freshly picked lilacs that stood in vases on the windowsill and the coffee table. Katie's world, he thought, his heart wrenching with fear for her. Her beautiful world filled with flowers, fairy tales, and untarnished ideals . . .

Katie awoke at seven, right on the button. Sleepily she rubbed her eyes and sat up. The note was no longer on the table, so she knew Taylor was home. Why hadn't he woken her? Her heart picked up in cadence and she moved across the sunlit room to the bedroom where the door was ajar. Taylor's snores punctuated the stillness, and Katie smiled wistfully. Her heart expanded with such incredible joy that she was momentarily suffocated.

Taylor lay on his stomach. Both pillows were on the floor, and he was sprawled out over half the bed, with no covers on him. His dark hair feathered across his brow, and his features were relaxed in deep sleep. Katie's heart mushroomed as she spotted her note in his closed fist. She ached to go to him, slip into bed next to him, ask him to love her. Katie closed her eyes, realizing that this wasn't the time. Not yet. She had sensed how fragile Taylor was—how confused about his divorce and about his feelings for her. Quietly she slipped into the room to retrieve a fresh dress for the day. Taylor wanted her, but he respected himself— and her—enough to wait. Katie found that endearingly old-fashioned, yet it was a quality she would want in the man with whom she fell in love.

Katie moved carefully to the closet, trying not to bump into anything. She had no idea when Taylor had come in, but the way he was sleeping, she suspected it was late. This morning, she would try to be extra quiet. A tough order for a clumsy Sagittarian! She smiled, feeling brilliant and alive as the sunlight that flooded her bedroom.

"Katie girl," Maud greeted her. The older woman, dressed in a Hawaiian print Muumuu, was seated on the floor in the midst of a stack of newly arrived books.

"Hi, Maud. What are you doing down there? You know we made an agreement: You work on your feet, I work on my knees. I'm younger than you."

Maud's grin widened. "You're looking fit this morning, Katie." Katie smiled. She had dressed in a bright red peasant blouse, a pink sash, and a purple skirt with white sandals.

Still smiling, she placed fresh bouquets of lilacs on each of the reading tables. "I had a wonderful day yesterday, Maud."

"Humph, you mean Taylor Grant finally made up for all the grief he's caused you?" Maud slowly rose from her knees.

Color stained Katie's cheeks as she put lilacs on the last table. "You still don't like him, do you?"

"I didn't say that," Maud said, seating herself behind the desk.

"Ouch!" Katie collided with a stack of books, then reached down to retrieve them. Her big toe smarted from the impact. "What *do* you think of him, Maud?"

"He's a reporter."

Katie put the books on the desk, giving Maud a distressed look. "He has also apologized, and is trying to rectify things."

"That's in his favor."

The hint of a smile appeared on Maud's face. "Look at me!" Katie demanded.

Maud lifted her head, barely about to contain her grin.

"Aha!" Katie cried. "Just as I thought: You do like him!"

"I think it's more important if *you* like him," Maud replied, a lively twinkle in her brown eyes.

Katie sighed and rested against the desk. "He's wonderful, Maud..."

"But not perfect."

"No...but then, who among us is? He's been deeply hurt by his divorce. He's afraid to reach out to love again..."

"Welcome to the real world."

Katie laughed, placing her hand on Maud's shoulder. "You just pretend to be old and crochety!"

Maud patted Katie's hand and nodded, her face softening. "He's not such a bad guy."

Brightening, Katie nodded. She looked at the wall clock. It was nearly eight, time to open. Already she saw several reporters waiting. "I like him, Maud. A lot."

"I know you do, lamb. Now, listen to me! You've got a busy schedule today. This afternoon you'll be at Dr. Abrams's veterinary hospital from two o'clock on. He called about it yesterday. He's got a whole slew of animals that need you."

"And we have to do inventory tonight, don't we?" Katie hated inventory.

"Afraid so." Maud glared at the reporters outside. "If I can get those pesky reporters out of here, I'll start this afternoon." She winked at Katie. "Maybe we can get a head start."

Katie glumly agreed. Numbers and figures weren't her thing. If it weren't for Maud's keen eye, she'd never be able to keep the accounting straight. Her mind moved to a more pleasant thought: that Taylor was asleep upstairs. Suddenly, despite the thought of inventory, and despite the reporters outside, Katie felt happier than she had in a long time.

Taylor pried one eye open, then the other. Soft classical music floated through the apartment, and he rolled over. Noon. It was noon! With a growl, he rolled out of bed and sat up, rubbing his stubbly face.

"Ahh, you're up."

He raised his head. Katie stood in the doorway, wearing a bright green apron and holding a wooden spoon in one hand. Automatically, he felt himself harden in need. She looked so clean and pretty!

"Barely," he muttered. "Why'd you let me sleep so long? I've got to get to the office."

"What a grouch! Guess I'd better watch it!" She laughed and walked to the bathroom, turning the faucets in the tub. "Come on, a nice hot bath will do wonders."

How could Katie be cheery when Taylor felt like a sodden lump? Sluggishly, he rose.

"You wouldn't have any coffee in the house, would you?"

"You think vegetarians don't drink coffee?" she teased. "I'll make some. How do you like it?"

"Black and strong," he muttered.

Katie held her tongue after this—Taylor didn't seem up to repartee. Her heart went out to him. "Coffee coming up," she promised.

"When it's ready, bring it in to me, Katie, please?"

"You got it. Are you hungry?"

"I don't even know if I'm alive yet."

He was shaving when Katie knocked lightly at the door. "Come on in," he called. Ouch! Dammit, he had cut himself again. Taylor glared into the steamy mirror.

Katie opened the door and entered. She set the mug of

coffee on the porcelain basin. "Looks like you cut yourself."

"Don't rub it in," he muttered, looking around for something to press against his latest wound.

Katie tried to ignore the masculine body, clad only in a towel wrapped haphazardly at the waist. "Hold still," she said and lightly applied her fingertips to the cut on his jaw.

Taylor's hooded eyes widened as he felt the intense heat from her touch. A tingling sensation seemed to focus in on his jaw, and he stood very still.

"Being the personal friend of a healer has certain benefits," she teased. "When I was a kid and cut my finger or scraped my knee, I'd always run to my mother so she could touch me. She always took away the pain, and that was all I cared about. Well, that should do it." She looked at the small cut, satisfied. "There's your coffee. By the time you're through in here, you ought to be awake." She turned around and left.

"I'll be damned," Taylor muttered, touching his jaw. It felt funny, the tingling sensation slowly dissolving from the locus of his injury. Taking a towel, he wiped steam from the mirror to look closely at the cut. His bloodshot eyes widened slightly. What had once been a deep gash was now a faint pink mark. His pupils dilated, and he angled his jaw closer to the mirror. Impossible! He'd been bleeding seconds before! Katie had applied no direct pressure to the cut. He dropped his hands to the sink, staring down at the basin. Confusion overwhelmed him momentarily. Grabbing the mug of coffee, he burned his tongue as he took a huge swallow.

"Katie—" He thrust open the bathroom door.

"Take a seat, Taylor. Lunch is ready." She pointed toward the living room.

Reluctantly Taylor made way as she picked up a tray filled with unknown things that smelled awfully good. He grimaced as he finished knotting his tie, and followed her.

"Look, we've got to talk."

"Aren't you hungry? I'm starved! I missed breakfast this morning." Quickly she arranged two plates with silverware and bright pink linen napkins. Next she brought over two huge pillows and gestured for him to sit down.

Taylor surveyed the meal as he sat cross-legged opposite her. "What is it?"

"Typical Scorpio. What's in it? What's it made of? Will it poison me?" She laughed softly and filled his plate, then handed it to him. "To answer your question. We have long-grain brown rice, fresh snow peas slightly steamed, and a fresh tomato sauce with eggplant, onion, green pepper, and mushrooms. Vegetarian spaghetti sauce. Satisfied?"

He had the good grace to look embarrassed. "I don't usually get home-cooked meals. I guess I'm a lousy guest, right?"

Katie poured herself a small glass of white wine. "Wrong. I'm glad you're curious about what I've made for you."

She was so precious! Taylor nearly reached out to touch her blazing cheek and tell her so. "Are you always so cheerful?"

"It's noon, Taylor, not six in the morning."

"You know, you're right." And cautiously, he tasted each of the foods on his plate.

Katie suppressed a giggle as she watched Taylor. The surprise showed in his eyes when he found the food palatable. "Well, do I pass muster as a cook?"

His mouth was full, so he nodded.

Trying to not say anything, Katie watched him gulp down two platefuls of food in fifteen minutes flat. He ate like a starved man; it was bad for his digestion. Katie eyed the last of the rice as he shoveled it onto his plate.

"Want some more?" he asked, before emptying the bowl.

"No, I'm stuffed. Go ahead."

"This is great, Katie. Thank you."

"So you're no longer antivegetarian?"

Taylor grinned. "I owe you an apology, don't I?"

"No, not really. You were hungry."

"Being diplomatic?"

"Trying to be."

"I was starved. I didn't eat last night because of the haz-mat spill. When I got home at three this morning, I was dead on my feet, I took a shower and was out like a light." His eyes grew thoughtful, and he held her gaze. "Thanks for leaving me the bed."

"I couldn't see destroying your back by forcing you to sleep on that settee."

Taylor smiled and leaned back, feeling thoroughly sated and relaxed. "Your cooking sure beats the hell out of the fast-food joints I've patronized for the last seven years. Covering the crime beat at night'll do that to you. I'd grab a doughnut and a cup of coffee. Sometimes I'd eat once in twelve hours. I'd be either too beat to eat or just too busy." He shrugged. "Maybe," he said thoughtfully, "just *maybe* California's okay. It's a special sort of place. Or maybe it's just you, Katie Riordan."

She felt heat rise to her cheeks. Nervous beneath his smoldering appraisal, she moved to gather the dishes.

"Don't go," Taylor said, his fingers stilling her hand.

Katie sat back, tucking her hands in her lap. "I'm going to have to leave in a few minutes. Maud wants to go to lunch."

"I understand. Listen, what's your schedule this afternoon?"

She took a deep breath. "Dr. Abrams needs me at the veterinary hospital this afternoon."

"Mind if I come along?"

"For your story on me?"

"Yes. I'll want to take pictures, too. Barry's off today, so I'll do it myself. Is that all right?"

She shrugged. "As long as Dr. Abrams doesn't mind, I don't."

He gave her a rueful look and touched the spot on his jaw where the cut had been. "You really shocked the hell out of me, Katie."

"I didn't mean to." She chewed on her lower lip. "Automatic reflex, I guess. I saw the blood and wanted to help you."

Taylor shook his head. "I can't understand what you do, Katie. The cut is healed. The world I come from, that's an impossibility."

"I know," she said softly.

"And yet, you did it."

She moved uncomfortably beneath his inspection. "You're making me feel like a bug under a microscope."

"I don't mean to, Katie. The look you see in my eyes is awe, not curiosity. Okay?"

A rush of relief went through her, and she nodded. "I can't stand being treated like a freak, Taylor. I'm not. We all have gifts. Healing happens to be mine, that's all."

He got to his feet and pulled her after him. Uncertainty was written on her face; he leaned down to kiss her lightly on the mouth.

"You never seemed like a freak to me, Katie," he told her quietly, holding her wide, trusting gaze. "Every hour I spend with you, I realize just how truly special and unique you are. One of a kind." My kind . . . but he couldn't say that. Not yet. Did Katie feel as strongly about him as he did about her? Did she know that one glance from those lapis lazuli eyes sent a shaft of longing straight through to his soul? Did she know one of her effervescent smiles lifted his dark, brooding spirits into the light? His hands tightened on her shoulder, and he yearned to kiss her hard and long, to carry her into that wonderfully romantic bedroom of hers and show her just how much she had come to mean to him.

Deviltry lurked in her eyes as she eased from his grip. "We'll see what you really think of me, Mr. Grant—after you see what I do at Dr. Abrams's clinic."

He matched her grin, helping her pick up the dishes. "You've got a deal, Ms. Riordan."

"Katie! Come in!" Dr. Lionel Abrams rose from his desk as Katie and Taylor entered the air-conditioned office. The veterinarian was in his early forties, lean, and wearing a white jacket.

"Hi, Lionel. I'd like you to meet a friend of mine, Taylor Grant. He's a reporter."

Dr. Abrams's smile disappeared while he gave Taylor the once-over. "Yes, I read his article about you, Katie."

Taylor gripped the vet's hand, noticing that Dr. Abrams had a firm handshake. "I'm in the process of trying to atone for that article, Doctor. I want to present the other side. That's why I'm here." He pointed to his tape recorder. "With your permission, Doctor, I'd like to photograph Katie touching your patients. And I'd also like to tape the session."

Abram's long face sobered, and he glanced at Katie. "It's up to you. I can't say I was impressed by Mr. Grant's analysis of your talent, Katie."

She placed her hand on the vet's arm. "It's all right, Lionel. Taylor is here to learn, this time."

The vet was skeptical, but he relented. He asked his assistant to provide them with white smocks. He looked over at Taylor as he led them through a side door.

"Katie comes here twice a week. She treats the animals —including those scheduled for surgery."

"I see." Taylor looked impressed. "And how long has she been doing this, Dr. Abrams?"

The vet smiled at Katie who walked at his side down the tiled hall. "Let's see, four and a half years now, I believe."

"And how did you hear of Katie?"

Dr. Abrams's eyes crinkled as he smiled. He held open the door to the room where animal cages were kept. "Actually, I went to her bookstore to search for a book on Bach Flower Remedies. At the time, Katie didn't realize I was a vet. When I saw this troop of people, most of them elderly, bringing in their pets, I decided to hang around and see what was happening." He stopped at the first cage, which contained an orange cat, and opened the door. He handed the cat to Katie. "I asked if I could stay and watch what she did, and she agreed. So I spent an amazing hour in her back room. I noticed one thing immediately: Every animal she touched became more alert and energetic. These pets were more than just animals to the elderly people who owned them; they were companions. Katie knew that; she was clearly sensitive to it. And I was impressed with her ability to handle both people and animals."

Taylor watched as Katie held the orange tomcat. Its ear appeared to have been all but chewed off in a recent fight. Taylor decided to take a couple of photographs. At his request the vet moved to stand beside Katie.

"Tell me, Doctor, did you believe in Katie's healing ability?"

"Her gift? Of course."

"Why 'of course'?"

"Because any doctor or nurse who genuinely loves his patients—animal or human—is in the business of healing, Mr. Grant. One of my instructors at Ohio State University had hands like Katie. I saw some pretty miraculous things there at the vet college."

"So you accept this phenomenon?"

Dr. Abrams gave him a pained look. He took the cat from Katie. "It's a gift."

"All right. What determines this gift, Doctor?"

Abrams shrugged and moved to the next cage. He extracted a small, furry white kitten with a bandaged front leg. "God decides. I certainly don't."

"Is it genetic? Katie says her mother had the same heal-ing touch."

"Could be." Dr. Abrams held up his splayed fingers and grinned at Katie. "I wish *I* had it. But all I'm good for is cutting and sewing."

"That's not true, Lionel!" Katie objected, stroking the green-eyed kitten. It purred madly in her arms. She glanced over at Taylor, the pop of the flashbulb blinding her momentarily. "He has the ability to heal, too. He just won't admit it."

Taylor put down the camera and drew out his notepad. He had the tape recorder running, but wanted to jot down a few of his ideas.

"I don't have the same energy Katie does," Lionel cor-rected.

"What do you mean?"

The vet studied his hands. "Most people with ability experience either a powerful tingling, or a warmth which passes through their fingers. I get only the barest hint of a tingle, nothing more. I've tried, believe me. My touch does not alter the condition of a scratch or bruise, or cure a headache." He looked over at Katie fondly. "Now, this lit-tle lady can take away a headache, stop bleeding, and heal surgical incisions. I can remove stitches sooner because of her."

"So, from your perspective, what Katie does is normal? An everyday event?"

"Of course. The important thing is that my animals get well swiftly and with a minimum of suffering."

Taylor smiled. "Most doctors don't quite see things your way."

"Plenty," Dr. Abrams agreed. "But so what? Look, Mr. Grant. What Katie does isn't odd or unusual. The general public is simply uninformed. Healing isn't magic. We don't understand quite how it works, but I suppose we will eventually. Soon the medical establishment will investigate people like Katie, and they'll learn that gifts like hers are positive and productive."

Taylor followed them around the spotless air-conditioned room. He took before and after photos of the animals Katie held. In each case, the animal became more active, its eyes brighter and more alert, following her touch. Well, Taylor couldn't blame them. He'd like to be stroked and patted by Katie, too. He noted that the amount of time she spent with her hands on an animal varied.

"How do you know when to stop?" he asked her.

Katie had her hand on a huge, gray Irish wolfhound. "The heat stops flowing through my fingers. That's when I take my hand away."

"Who controls this stopping and starting?"

"Not I. I try to keep my mind blank when I'm working. But you don't have to. I can carry on a conversation, as I'm doing now, and the energy flows just the same."

Dr. Abrams glanced at Taylor. "Katie once explained that a healer is like a piece of tubing. Her body is simply a conduit through which the energy flows."

"But where does this energy come from?" Taylor pressed.

The vet shrugged and looked up at the ceiling. "Katie calls it the cosmos. I call it God. I'm sure others have other ideas." He smiled slightly. "How can you put a name on love? That's what this unseen energy really is, in my opinion: love, need, compassion, a desire to help a suffering fellow being. The healer is the vehicle for this energy."

"You're talking a lot of philosophy and very little evidence, Doctor."

Katie looked up. "You're seeing the invisible side of physics at work right now, Taylor."

She removed her hand from the wolfhound, patting his head. The dog thumped his long whiplike tail. She smiled.

"Is that it for today?"

"Not quite, Katie. I've got a cat that was hit by a truck

yesterday. Its skull was caved in above his eyes. I really don't think he's going to make it. But the cat belongs to a blind boy and he's distraught over the loss of his friend . . ."

Taylor saw the sudden anguish in Katie's face, as if she were assuming the boy's pain. They followed the vet to a large cage where the gray and black striped cat lay. The animal was unconscious; an I.V. was attached to his bandaged rear leg.

"Now, what I've done so far is to relieve the skull pressure from the cat's brain. But the brain could be bruised or even hemorrhaging and that will cause death, too."

"I see," Katie whispered. Gently, she placed her left hand lightly on the cat's shoulder.

"I was up every two hours last night to see how he was doing. At three this morning, he went into a convulsion so I added an anticonvulsant drug to the I.V."

Taylor took a photo. "Doctor, what are this cat's chances of surviving?"

"One in a hundred."

Taylor sat at his desk, rereading his article a third time, occasionally editing the glowing green text on the screen of the word processor. He had another hour of work to do, but he wanted to go home. Home to Katie and her apartment. Funny, Taylor mused, that in two weeks' time, his entire life had been turned upside down by Katie and her world.

He stared at the screen, not really seeing it at all. Katie and her world. More and more, it was his world, too. The threatening phone calls had not stopped, and he didn't feel comfortable leaving Katie alone. He had never mentioned the prowler he'd seen at the door to her store, but he'd talked her into changing her locks to stronger ones. With a sigh, he got up, moving to the dented percolator. He smiled: If Katie knew how much coffee he'd consumed, she'd hit the roof. For all intents and purposes, she'd nearly turned him into a damned vegetarian. But she was a great cook, and he'd do damn near anything for a home-cooked meal, he was discovering. He'd even acquiesced to her demand that he help with the cooking. Now he could turn out a halfway decent rabbit food meal, too.

By now, though, Katie would have eaten. She would have taken her lilac-scented bath and would be playing the piano—as she did every evening after work. And Lord—could she play! How many times had Taylor sat there in the evening, herbal tea in hand (instead of coffee), listening to her play classics from memory! He and Katie had grown incredibly close. And it took every shred of his control not to move beyond that barrier he had placed between them.

Sitting back down, Taylor stared at the screen. To hell with it! He wanted to go home to Katie. He printed out a copy of his article; he wanted her to read it. He picked up a set of photos, then stopped to stare at one of them, an odd smile on his face. The cat with the head injury had lived. In another week, he'd be going home to the little blind boy who waited anxiously for his friend. Taylor made a mental note to have Barry go over to the boy's home and take photographs of the reunion.

Katie flew to the door as Taylor closed it behind him. His exhaustion disappeared at the sound of her throaty laugh. She threw her arms around his neck and kissed him soundly. He juggled his briefcase and camera, then took a step back to steady both of them.

"Hey . . . what's this for?" he asked, sliding his free arm around her to hold her tight against him. Lord, she felt good! So alive . . . He closed his eyes, burying his face in the fragrant mass of her newly washed hair.

"I missed you!"

"Made two of us."

"I was worried."

"I wanted to finish the article about you, Katie." He

released her, shutting the door. Glancing at the phone he asked, "Any more calls?"

She stepped away, dressed in a pale lavender granny gown sprigged with tiny violets. "There were only two today."

"Did he say the same thing?"

"Same thing," she said, watching as he put his jacket in the closet. Usually, Taylor would come and have lunch with her; today he hadn't, and Katie had missed his company even more than usual. "Are you hungry?"

"Starved. What kind of rabbit food do you have in store for today?" he teased, taking her into his arms and lifting her off her bare feet.

Katie clung to him, her laughter childlike as he whirled her around three times. Every day, Taylor was allowing her to see more and more of his real self. No longer was he her brooding dark knight. He smiled often, and she melted beneath the gaze that smoldered with raw hunger for her. She kissed his nose, his eyes, and finally molded her lips to his strong male mouth, finding utter pleasure there.

"Mmmm," she whispered, "you're my advance dessert."

He stared into her lustrous blue eyes and swallowed hard, wildly aware of her slender body pressed close to him. "Just being around you is my dessert, princess." Lord, how he wanted her! Taylor gently let her down and kept his arm around her as she led him to the kitchen.

Katie curled up on the settee with his article while he ate a late makeshift lunch. A softened smile touched her lips, and she returned her attention to his story. Finally she had finished it and allowed her hands to rest on the sheaf of papers.

"Well? What do you think?"

"I think it's terribly one-sided."

"Slanted," he corrected. "Why not? The first story was slanted, too."

"But is that good journalism?"

"This is a human-interest piece. It's okay to editorialize in such cases. I make it quite clear to the reader where I'm coming from. It's fine, sweetheart."

Her eyes grew warm. "I like it. I can feel the emotions coming through in your words." She picked up the black-and-white photos. "And these show great care and sensitivity on your part."

Taylor rose and came to sit down beside her, his face grave as he studied her. "You do like it, then?"

"Of course I do. I love it. Maybe now people won't be so afraid of me and what I do."

He took an ebony curl and wound it gently around his finger. "There were a lot of things I wanted to put in that article but didn't, Katie."

She lifted her eyes to meet his, yearning to move into his arms, to love him. "Like what?" She gave him an impish smile. "Such as: she's a scatterbrain who can't walk three feet without bumping into something. She's terrible at math and even worse at inventory. She can never find her keys. Did you want to say that if you hadn't helped me with the account books, and found a three thousand dollar error in *my* favor, I'd have missed a mortgage payment?"

Taylor smiled slightly, inhaling her special fragrance, entranced by her lips as they formed the words. "No," he said quietly, leaning over to place a feathery kiss on the velvet slope of her cheek. "I wanted to tell the world how you've changed me in the past three weeks. That healing is more than just the laying on of hands. You've transformed my life, too."

Katie quivered beneath the gentle assault of his kisses, her eyes closing, a sigh escaping as she leaned back, allowing him to continue his foray down her neck. Automatically, she placed her hands against his chest, feeling the beat of his heart beneath her palms. His moist breath trailed along the open V of her dress, and she felt her nipples grow taut.

"I wanted to tell them how you brought sunlight back into my gloomy existence, how you made me smile again," he went on, sliding his fingers into her wealth of hair. Gently he massaged her scalp. Her moan of pleasure went through him like molten lava as she gave herself to his ministrations. "And that your laughter lifts me, your smile melts me, and your touch . . ." He ran his tongue across her exposed collarbone. "Your touch," he breathed thickly, "makes me starve for you."

Taylor sat up, allowing her time to assimilate what he had said, aware that her half-closed eyes were bright with pleasure. It made him feel good to know he could please her. He had never known how to please Mary Ann. Katie responded to each caress, to each minute touch he bestowed. He was in awe of their chemistry; it exploded into a raging fire each time they came close to each other.

Taylor held his breath. He watched Katie languish in the passion that spun between them like gold eiderdown. He wondered if she knew what he was asking of her: He wanted to take her to bed tonight. To love her. Make her his . . . share the magic that always simmered around them. Marry her . . . Fear clashed with need. Would she reject him? Mary Ann had . . . Taylor froze inwardly, afraid of what her answer would be . . .

Chapter 10

KATIE SLID HER fingers around Taylor's neck, following his hairline. There was invitation in her lapis eyes. "I'd like to add a few things to your article, too," she began, her voice tremulous. "That you've given me sunlit days"—she drew him forward, placing her lips against his mouth—"and rainbow nights. Take me to our bed, Taylor darling. Love me, let me share with you."

She no longer cared that Taylor might leave her life just as abruptly as he had entered it. She knew he had been deeply wounded by Mary Ann. Perhaps he would never truly recover. But she wanted to reach out, touch, and become a part of whatever was left within Taylor. And as he lifted her into his arms and carried her into the darkness of the bedroom, Katie wanted nothing more of life than this exquisite moment with him.

Taylor couldn't believe it. He hadn't even had to ask!

There were thirty tiny pearl buttons on her gown, and he sat, his fingers trembling, as he patiently freed each one. He never once allowed his gaze to leave hers. Katie reached up to unbutton his shirt.

"I'm shaking," she said.

"Me, too."

With a laugh, she cradled Taylor's face between her hands, savoring the sandpaper quality of his evening beard. "I know it's not out of fear."

"Need," he said thickly. "I need you, Katie, like I've never needed another woman." The last button gave way. Taylor took her hands, kissing each palm, running his tongue across the small calluses there.

Jolts of pleasure sped through Katie. Taylor released her hands, and she took a shaky breath. His fingers moved, scaldingly hot, across her collarbones, sliding the thin cotton from her shoulders and urging the sleeves from her arms.

"Beautiful," he said hoarsely, cupping her small breasts, "you're perfect, Katie, perfect for me . . ." He bent to sample the dusky nipples that hardened as he caressed her breasts . . .

Katie lay back, liquid fire radiating from throbbing nipples that begged to be captured and seduced by his knowing tongue. Each gentle tug made her moan, and instinctively she arched toward him, wanting him to join her on the bed. Her breath came in shallow gasps as he reluctantly left her side. Barely raising her lashes, she watched as Taylor stepped out of his clothes. Light from the living room spilled quietly through the open door, and she marveled at the hard, unforgiving planes of his body. He was ruggedly beautiful, and she longed to run her hands over him, worship him, and tell him how beautiful he was, in her eyes and heart . . .

She opened her arms to receive him. His chest was warm and hard as she ran her fingers across the expanse, the hair a wiry carpet beneath her palm. Katie looked up into his hooded eyes, her lips parting with invitation.

"I wonder if anyone has told you how beautiful you are," she whispered faintly, her voice growing husky as he trailed his hand lightly across her thigh and hip. "My beautiful dark knight, who bears a wounded heart." And she rose on one elbow, pressing small kisses on his chest. A groan reverberated through him, and Katie thrilled to his response. Emboldened, she gently guided him to his back and continued to kiss him, caressing each nipple. He gripped her hard by the shoulders, his breath escaping through clenched teeth.

Suddenly Katie found herself lying beneath him, staring up into stormy eyes fraught with desire, burning with fierce intensity. "I want to please you," she murmured, running her fingers across his powerful shoulders.

"You do. Always," he said. "Let me please you now, Katie. Let me show you how much you mean to me, how much you've given me already."

She smiled. "Show me, beloved dark knight." And she closed her eyes, waiting for the kiss that came seconds later. His mouth radiated sensual power, cajoling her to return the passion that inflamed her senses. As his hands followed the curve of her, she arched against him, crying out his name, begging him, needing him. He tore his mouth from hers, teasing her nipples with his tongue until she writhed with mindless pleasure beneath him. An ache, centered in her lower body, turned to raw hunger. She sobbed his name as his hand sought and found the core of her, sliding downward to her liquid center. Dazed with the onslaught of his fiery kisses, lifted on a shimmering veil of exquisite need, she felt him draw her thighs apart and she waited . . . waited . . .

He pressed himself inside her. She was a tight glove surrounding him, drowning him in the sweetness of herself. A groan tore from deep within Taylor, and he froze, holding Katie tightly, afraid in his hunger that he had hurt her. Sweat rolled off his brow, trailing down the line of his clenched jaw. He was wildly aware of her scent, her responsive form beginning to move slowly beneath him, inviting him to share the love they had withheld from each other for too long. Taylor kissed her damp brow, her long lashes, and finally her parted lips. She tasted like wildflower honey, and he moved his hips, listening to the sigh of pleasure that rose from her slender throat.

Katie felt him holding back, and she met and matched his cautious rhythm. She wasn't fragile; she was a woman who loved him without reserve, and she allowed her desire to flare to life within her as she gently assaulted him with kisses meant to shatter the last of his control. His mouth was strong and male, and she nipped and soothed his lips with her tongue. He quivered, and she smiled to herself, deepening the kiss, thrusting her tongue between his teeth. A shudder wound through him, and she relaxed as he gripped her hips, drawing her to him. Heat uncoiled through Katie, and she arched like a taut bow as heat melded with light and she splintered into million dancing, dappled lights across the surface of the universe he had just given her.

Moments later, Katie felt Taylor tense. A growl, fierce and low, tore from him. She moved with him, giving him pleasure as he had given pleasure to her. Taylor fell beside her, breathing heavily, his arm wrapped protectively around her, pulling her close, never letting her go. She kissed his glistening face, tasting the salt of his perspiration, feeling the spikiness of his lashes beneath her lips and the maleness of his mouth. Weakly, he opened his eyes, staring darkly up at her.

"You're a figment of my imagination," he rasped, his hand coming to rest on her cheek. "You've got to be."

Katie rested her head on his chest. His heart pounded

hard beneath her ear. She smiled as his arms went around her. "Why do you say that?"

Taylor managed a half-laugh, consumed with the languor that only good loving could bring. "You felt so damn good. I feel good."

She laughed with him, joy surrounded her. "Flight of the unicorn," she murmured, sliding her hand across his chest.

"Unicorn? What does the unicorn have to do with any of this?" Taylor teased, stroking her ebony hair.

"Unicorns stay only if there is love given." She smiled and closed her eyes. "What you just gave me made me feel as if I had been flung into a universe of exploding stars. I felt so light, so wonderfully fulfilled. Just like a unicorn would . . ."

"That's just one more thing I love about you, Katie," he murmured. "Your wild, unfettered imagination. To you, nothing is impossible. To me, little is possible. Or was. You've changed all that." Taylor ran his hand lightly across the curve of her delicate back, drying it with the palm of his hand. "You're the unicorn, Katie. You're love. Don't you know that?"

Tears pricked her eyes. She put her hands on his chest and studied him in the darkness. "No less than you are, Taylor. Why do you think you have no love to give in return? Look at what you just gave me. I've never felt so happy. Or so complete."

Taylor saw the glimmer of tears in her luminous eyes. "Crystal tears from sapphire eyes. Tell me, princess. Are they tears of pity for me?"

She kissed him tenderly. "I'd never pity you, Taylor. In my heart, I feel the pain you carry." She stroked his chest where his heart lay. "I only want to take some of that pain from you and replace it with good feelings."

He framed her face with his hands, drowning in her

innocent, vulnerable eyes. He was shaken by her trust in him; she gave him everything without reserve. "I don't feel pain anymore, Katie. Just the happiness we create."

She sniffed, and the tears spilled down her cheeks. "That's more than I ever dreamed of."

Taylor kissed her longingly, wanting to absorb her completely into his heart and soul. "And you're the one who said dreams always come true," he murmured against her lips.

"I dared to dream even beyond my limits, when it came to you and me," she admitted in a whisper, caressing his mouth tenderly.

He inhaled her feminine fragrance, content to lie with her on top of him, their mouths touching. "Keep dreaming for both of us, then, Katie. Because I'm beyond anything I'd ever imagined for us. And believe me, I imagined plenty."

She smiled and nuzzled his jaw, content. "The flight of the unicorn infuses you with love. And then it laps outward like waves on an ever-widening cosmic ocean," she murmured. "That's what we shared, my beautiful dark knight with the soul of poet and the heart of a unicorn." Her lashes drooped closed and in moments, she spiraled into a dream world of brilliant colors—with Taylor at her side.

Taylor jerked awake. It was still dark. His heart was beating hard, as though he were in fright. What had wakened him? Worried, he glanced at Katie who slept soundly at his side, her hand thrown across his belly. He lay still, realizing he was drenched in cold sweat. Why? He switched his attention to his ears. Had a sound jarred him out of sleep? Only the faint hum of the clock on his bedstand could be heard. He twisted his head to look at it: 2:00 A.M.

Must have been a bad dream, Taylor thought, relaxing. He drew Katie closer and pulled up the sheet to cover them. She snuggled next to him, and he smiled, a ribbon of happiness threading through him, dissolving the fear he had felt earlier. Still . . . he lay for a long time, just listening. Could the intruder be back? Was he trying to jimmy the downstairs lock? Had he sneaked up the stairs to force the lock on the apartment door? All manner of ugly possibilities haunted him. Were the intruder and her caller one and the same man? He didn't know, and the fear and frustration ate at him. Why couldn't the police pin down that damn caller? Partly because he never stayed on the phone long enough to be traced.

The longer he stayed awake, the harder Taylor found it to focus on the problem. Katie was in his arms; she was his, and the knowledge made him feel whole. He was needed and wanted. And Taylor had to laugh at himself, because he had always thought himself so self-sufficient. With Katie, every day was a living miracle. Instead of the sullen fights with Mary Ann, he had Katie's effervescent self, her goofy yet endearing moods, the unique way in which she saw the world. It made him feel like living once again. He turned to kiss her forehead, inhaling her special lilac scent. "I love you," he told her softly, and the darkness surrounding them absorbed his words.

The phone was ringing. Taylor mumbled an oath. Katie stirred. Faint sunlight lanced through the sheer green panels that hung over the bed. She didn't want to leave Taylor's arms. But the phone wouldn't quit ringing, and finally Katie forced open her eyes and threw off the sheet.

"Damn reporters," Taylor growled.

"I'll get it," she told him, rubbing her eyes. What time was it? Only six-thirty in the morning? They could have had another hour of sleep! Katie stumbled out into the living room.

"Hello?" she said, her voice sleepy.

"Three days and you're dead."

Katie froze. The phone line clicked and then began to hum. It was the same man. Before, he had only threatened. Now he was setting a deadline. A chill knifed through Katie; her hands went clammy.

"Katie?" Taylor called. "Who is it?"

Three days and you're dead.

"Katie?" He staggered out of bed, sensing something was wrong. He brushed the hair from his brow and moved into the living room. His brain was barely working; instinct took over. She stood with her back to him, the phone in her hand. In four strides he was at her side.

"The threatening caller?" he asked, taking the phone from her and replacing the receiver. Her fingers were icy, and he spun her around. Taylor was unprepared for the naked fear in her expression.

"What did he say? Katie? Talk to me."

"H-he said I had three days and then I'd die," she choked out, blindly moving into his arms.

He wanted to curse. But that wouldn't help Katie as she trembled in his embrace. "Was it the same man?"

"Yes. Taylor, he's so evil. I-I could feel his hatred over the phone. Why does he hate me so much? I don't under-stand . . ."

"I don't either, princess. Come on, let's get some clothes on. Will you make me some coffee so I can wake up?"

"Yes."

Taylor squeezed her and kissed her tousled hair. "I'm going down to the police station. There's no excuse for their inaction. Why haven't they found that jerk by now? This is the first time he's threatened something that spe-cific. Or that sinister." He tried to minimize his own fear, to mask his anger. There was no need to upset Katie any more than she already was. The flow of adrenaline had dispelled his grogginess, and Taylor made a mental list of things to do today. He'd call Dean Gerus and tell him that until this crisis was resolved and Katie's pursuer was caught, he was on leave from his job. The editor-in-chief might fire him, but Taylor didn't give a damn at this point. If the cops wouldn't give Katie the help she deserved, he damn well would provide it.

Over coffee in the kitchen, Taylor told her, "You don't go anywhere without me, Katie. Understand? I want you to stay in this apartment with the door locked until I return. If you need me, I'll be at the police station."

Shakily, Katie rubbed her aching temple, unable to control the stress headache that had blossomed shortly after the threatening call. She had pulled on her lavender dress and gone through the motions of making coffee. She looked up at him. "How could everything be so beautiful one second and a nightmare the next?"

Taylor set his mug on the drainboard. "It's going to be okay, princess," he assured her, holding her tight against him. He pressed a line of kisses along her jaw until he found her warm and willing lips; he drowned in her sweetness. He wanted to protect her, tell her how much he loved her. But that would have to wait until this crisis passed. "I want to say so many things to you, Katie," he whispered. "I wanted to wake up this morning and love you all over again, this time slow and sweet."

She nuzzled his jaw, needing his strength more than ever before. The words, 'I love you,' nearly found their way to her lips, but Katie had resolved the evening before not to saddle Taylor with such feelings. He was still healing from the past. He didn't need any added pressure right now. She could wait, because in her heart she knew that if it was right, they would say those words to each other one day.

"Are you giving me a rain check?" she teased; but her attempt at humor was lame. Katie saw the concern in Taylor's narrowed gray eyes. She knew she couldn't protect herself from the threat issued by the caller. It wasn't because she was a woman; it was simply that her life experience had not prepared her for such an event. Taylor had lived with the violent side of life for a long time. He knew how criminals operated, far better than she . . .

"You've got it, princess." He kissed her once more, hard and swift. "I'll be back in an hour at the latest. Call Maud and let her open the bookstore for you. When I get back, you can go down and take over—unless the police want to talk to you. Okay?"

Glumly, Katie agreed.

"Now, look, Sergeant Johnson, I don't want any more runarounds. What about this situation with Katie Riordan?"

The sergeant, a man well into his fifties who wore a bulldog expression on his florid face, set his jaw. "And I told you before, Mr. Grant, the telephone company hasn't been able to trace those calls."

Taylor glared down at the overweight officer behind the desk. Typical small town cop, he thought angrily. He'd like to throw the squat, dumpy little man into a certain corner of the South Bronx for a week and see how he held up there. "The caller still hasn't stayed on the line long enough to get a trace?" he guessed, keeping a tight rein on his escalating anger.

"Right, and he's probably calling from different public phones." Johnson shoved a record of all the calls toward him. "You were in crime reporting, Grant. You know we can't zero in on whoever's doing it without a specific phone number to target. This guy's smart."

Taylor looked grudgingly through the data. The sergeant was right. "What about suspects? Surely you've got a profile on any crazies who stir up troubles here in Rio Conchos?"

Johnson shrugged his rounded shoulders and lit a cigarette. "Look, Grant, we're not going to put in extra man-hours at the taxpayers' expense. Not for some bookstore owner getting lousy crank calls."

Taylor stepped menacingly forward. "Now, you listen here, Johnson. Katie Riordan pays her taxes to this city, just like everybody else. And she deserves your concern and protection." Uttering a violent oath, Taylor slammed his hand down on the desk.

"Now you look here," Johnson sputtered, shocked by the reporter's unexpected attack.

"Someone wants to murder Katie Riordan. That's a hell of a lot more important, Johnson." Taylor punched his finger toward the policeman. "All right, Sergeant. If you won't help, then I'll demand access to police records, and I'll find some suspects. And when I do, I'm going to track them down myself. And then your people are going to check them out." He smiled savagely, his gray eyes glittering slits. "It's my right as a citizen to protect Katie, since you refuse to do your job. Believe me, when I get done with you and this two-bit department that calls itself a police station, the whole country is going to know how you operate."

Johnson sputtered, turning the color of a ripe plum. But he only watched as the reporter turned and headed into the room where records were kept.

Katie listened in silence as Taylor told her about his confrontation with the police. She had taken a bath and changed into an ankle-length peach skirt and white Victorian blouse. The orange belt emphasized her narrow waist. She tried to behave calmly, her fingers knotted in her lap, as she listened to Taylor's instructions.

"I'll take you downstairs now, Katie." He handed her a list of addresses gleaned from the police files. "I'm going to call you once an hour to see how you're doing. If you don't answer that phone, I'll be on my way back to the bookstore in an instant. If you see anyone who looks even remotely suspicious, call the police. Before I left there,

Johnson promised to send a patrol car out if you called."
He forced a smile, noting how pale she had become. "I'll
be back at noon, and we'll have lunch together."

Katie nodded jerkily. "Do you really think all these
elaborate precautions are necessary, Taylor? I mean, this
guy has been calling for weeks and he's done nothing."

Taylor gripped her elbow, guiding Katie to her feet. She
looked beautiful this morning, and Taylor wanted to tell
her so. Frustration ate at him; there was so much he wanted
to say to her and so little time! "We don't know if he is or
isn't, Katie. I'm not taking a chance that he isn't serious."
His voice trembled slightly as he led her to the door and
opened it. "I care for you too much to let anything happen
to you. You're the first decent thing to happen to me in a
decade, and I'll be damned if I'm going to risk your being
hurt by this jerk. Bear with me. I've got the names of five
men who are known to have made telephone threats in the
past. Four were recently released from mental hospitals.
The fifth is a convicted arsonist, out on parole. Maybe I
can turn up something with one of them. They all live in
Rio Conchos."

She gripped his hand. "Be careful."

Taylor smiled. Leaning down, he placed a tender kiss
on Katie's ripe lips. "I have you to come home to. I'll be
very careful."

Maud eyed Katie. "Girl, if you don't settle down,
you're going to wear yourself out," she warned gruffly. All
morning, Katie had been arranging books in alphabetical
order by subject as Taylor had suggested she do well over a
week ago. Today, Katie welcomed busywork.

She wiped the dust off her fingers with a towel and rose
from her knees.

The store was taking on a slicker look, a look that be-
spoke organization. That was Taylor's influence, Katie ac-

knowledged with a small smile. She went to the teakettle and placed it on the hot plate.

"I need some chamomile tea to settle my nerves," she told Maud.

"Make it two. My nerves are shot, too."

Katie glanced up in surprise because Maud seemed her normal, unflappable self. The older woman sat at the desk sorting order forms from a dozen or so different publishers; she seemed surrounded by a fortress of paper.

"What's your feeling about this telephone threat, Maud? You're always a good one for gut instinct."

"Humph! You ask me, this is serious. I'm glad Taylor is doing something, even if the lazy, good-for-nothing police department ain't!"

Katie smiled gently, setting out two china cups and saucers. It was the first time Maud had called Taylor by his first name. Clearly Maud was softening in her views. When the kettle began to whistle, Katie poured the boiling water into the cups, then added the tea bags. She brought the cups to the desk and leaned against it, cup in hand.

"I really care for him, Maud," she confided.

"Humph! That's been obvious for quite a while."

Katie's eyes sparkled. "Can't fool you, can I?"

"You weren't trying." Maud laughed and sipped at her tea contently. "At first, I didn't like Taylor Grant. He was out for himself, a real selfish type. Later, he changed." Maud looked around the bookstore. "When he started helping you get this place organized, I decided to sit back and watch. Listen. He didn't try to tell you how to run your place, Katie. He showed you different methods and left the decisions up to you. He's not as pushy and domineering as I first thought."

The warmth of the china cup felt good to her cool fingers, and Katie blew gently on the tea. "He's special to me, Maud."

"I know, lamb." Maud smiled up at her. "And it's obvious he feels the same way about you. I caught him looking at you plenty of times. He always had the most wistful look on his face . . . That hard face of his melted, Katie. You're good for him. He's good for you. Each of you has changed under the influence of the other."

"Taylor *has* mellowed."

"You could tell he was hurting bad by the way he behaved," Maud pointed out. "Being around you has changed him. He's more himself now, I'd venture. Not so hard. Not carrying that chip around on his shoulder anymore." The old woman chuckled. "He loves you, Katie girl."

Heat rushed to Katie's cheeks and she avoided Maud's twinkling brown eyes. "I'm not sure . . ."

"Well, I am!" Maud rubbed her hands together. "Ain't been around all this time not to be able to know love when I see it. Yes, I can hear those wedding bells ringing already."

Katie sat at her desk in the bookstore, preparing to lock up in half an hour. She wanted to close before it got very dark outside. She frowned and went to the door. There, to the west, was a huge, roiling mass of bruised clouds. Her eyes widened with happiness: a thunderstorm! During the five years she had lived in Rio Conchos, she had seen only three of them. They were rare in this area, she discovered, and she missed them acutely. She watched as the sky dimmed, the clouds advancing on the town like an army. She was glad she had sent Maud home at six, when Taylor left to track down the last of the five suspects.

Some of her fear had abated during the day. She had received no further threatening calls. Normally she got several each day. Had Taylor scared one of those five suspects so that the culprit stopped frightening her? She hoped so as she began her nightly accounting of the day's business.

But her mind refused to remain on the figures. Instead,

her gaze moved to a copy of the *Messenger,* a large area weekly. Taylor had brought it with him when they had shared a quick evening meal upstairs. His article and photos had been picked up by several syndicates and now were on the wires to other newspapers.

She heard the first warning rumble of thunder, far in the distance. The sky had turned inky in the dusk, and Katie saw streetlights going on down the block and people running for shelter. The storm would be brief, but Katie would enjoy the lightning display—she always did. And soon the engorged clouds would send their deluge earthward . . .

By eight o'clock the storm had passed. Sidewalks and road gleamed wetly in its aftermath. Katie got up and locked the door, turned the sign to Closed, and shut off the window display lights. The phone rang.

"Unicorn Bookshop."

"Is this the chief unicorn?"

Katie smiled and perched a hip on the desk, cradling the phone in her hand. "It is."

"Then I need you," Taylor said.

A shiver of desire coursed through her as his voice dropped to an intimate murmur. "You do?"

"Sure do."

"You must be hungry again."

"For you, princess. Only for you. Listen, I'm done for this evening."

"Did you find the fifth guy?"

"Yeah. Your typical sleaze-ball."

Katie shivered, wondering how Taylor could deal with such people. "What do you think?"

"None of these guys are stellar human beings," he answered dryly. "Any one of them could be your caller."

"Or maybe none."

"Right. Look, I'll be there in twenty minutes. How about if I treat my favorite lady unicorn to a hot fudge sundae at the Carousel Ice Cream Shoppe?"

Katie brightened. Taylor knew about her fondness for ice cream—the one non-health food she allowed herself —and she desperately wanted to put this whole sordid affair behind her, if only for a little while. "I'd love it!"

Taylor laughed. "There's no secret to pleasing you, is there, princess?"

She sobered, cradling the phone in both hands. "You please me, Taylor. You make me happy."

"I know...I didn't know dreams could come true, Katie. You're my dream, you know that."

"Hurry," she whispered, "I miss you so. I'll meet you upstairs. I'm closing the store now."

"Twenty minutes," he promised, "and I'll see you at the apartment."

She had no more than hung up the phone when the lights suddenly went out, leaving her in total darkness.

"Oh," she muttered, inching her way around the desk, "that darned storm." California didn't get many electrical storms. Katie speculated that an errant bolt of lightning had found its way to a transformer east of Rio Conchos, knocking out the electricity momentarily. Where was the flashlight? She knelt behind the desk, groping through each drawer. Where had she put it? Why hadn't she listened to Taylor? He had said to keep the flashlight in a handy place, or near the fuse box ...

"Candles ... that's it!" If she couldn't find a flashlight, she did know where the candles were: in the back classroom where people brought their pets to be healed. Katie got up, hands outstretched. With Taylor's help, they had completely rearranged the room, and she was still unfamiliar with the new layout. Twice she bumped into desks, bruising her hip. Katie rubbed the tender area, her attention swinging to the front door. She turned around. Through the plate windows in the door, she saw the dark shape of a man. Her heart picked up in cadence, and one hand moved to her throat. It couldn't be Taylor; barely three minutes had elapsed since his phone call.

Terror rooted Katie to the spot. She watched the man jerk savagely at the door. The glass shook in its frame. The man continued his powerful assault. Katie's eyes widened as she saw him back away and move to one of the display windows. Ice formed in her veins as she saw him light a rag that was stuffed into the mouth of the bottle in his hand. It was the caller! Oh, Lord, she had to escape! The back door was locked, and the key was in the desk. There was no way out except through the front door where her assailant stood. Panic clawed through Katie, and she screamed as the window erupted into jagged shards of glass. The Molotov cocktail sailed through . . .

The bottle landed just inside the window, fire erupting in sheets as the gasoline spread. Near hysteria, Katie ran back to the desk. There was sufficient light from the flames to illuminate her way. She tore a fingernail off, trying to open the middle drawer. The keys. The keys! A second scream caught in her throat as another Molotov cocktail came hurling through the window. Katie ducked, gagging and choking on the smoke as the fire spread quickly to the wall of books. Another explosion occurred behind her. Katie whirled around. She was now caught between two walls of flame!

Clenching the keys, Katie ran down the narrow aisle between the flames. Just as she made it to the rear classroom she tripped, striking her head on the edge of the desk. The keys slipped from her numbed fingers, and she sank to the carpet, unconscious. The fire continued its licking path across the carpet toward her . . .

Taylor's eyes widened as he pulled around the corner. A dull orange glow rose eerily against the darkness. Terror sheared through him as he slammed down the accelerator. The Trams Am screamed forward. Katie! Good Lord, the whole building was on fire! He saw fire engines streaking toward him. Their sirens wailed mournfully, their red and white lights stark against the wet pavement. The Trans Am squealed to a skidding stop, and Taylor leaped out, running hard down the sidewalk. People had started to gather, open-mouthed and stunned. The sirens grew closer and louder. Taylor tore off his jacket, holding it over his nose and mouth as he took the wooden stairs to Katie's apartment two at a time. Anguish stabbed through him. He'd seen too many fires, too many arson-related tragedies. Smoke could kill. Taylor coughed violently in the thick, heavy grayish smoke at the top of the stairs. Katie was inside! She could already be dead. Smoke and heat always rose during a fire. Had the fire eaten through the floor of her apartment yet? Was she alive?

"Katie!" he thundered and put his hand on the doorknob. He jerked his seared hand back. Locked! The door was locked! Hadn't he told her to keep it that way? Taylor sobbed for breath, digging frantically in his pocket for the key. It was dark, except for the flicker of the spreading fire below. He found the key and shoved it into the lock, his hand shaking badly.

He kicked the door open, keeping his jacket against his face. He screamed Katie's name again and again. No answer! The rooms filled with gathering smoke, and he hugged the walls as he searched for her. Sweat trickled into his eyes, already tearing heavily from the smoke. He gasped as he finished his search. Katie wasn't here. She'd said she would be! Had the man who threatened to kill Katie taken her from the apartment? Was she still in the bookstore?

Turning, Taylor heard the shouts of fire fighters. In moments, they'd be hosing down the raging inferno. He ran out of the apartment and tore down the stairs.

Huge white hoses looked like fat spaghetti, throbbing as hundreds of gallons of water surged through them. Taylor halted at the front of the bookstore; it was completely enveloped in sheets of flame. The back door! He raced among the running fire fighters as they began to spray the inferno. Keys in hand, Taylor ran to the rear of the building.

His eyes smarted and blurred as he worked the key into the stubborn lock. There! The door literally blew out of his hands, throwing him a good six feet backwards. Dazed, he crawled forward on hands and knees, shaking his head to clear it. He should have known better: heat buildup could cause windows to blow out and doors to explode. He held the jacket to his face, moving in low and fast beneath the smoke now roiling thickly out of the opening where the door had once been.

The heat was intense; his skin smarted. His right hand was badly blistered. Crawling on hands and knees, unable to see anything, Taylor screamed for Katie. He hugged the baseboard, knowing that if he got too far from the wall, he'd become disoriented. He could die, unable to find his way out again through the thick, cottony gray smoke . . .

Oh, Lord, please let her be alive. I love her . . . I love her.

"Katie!" he cried, choking badly as smoke clawed down his throat. The desk! He reached out and felt the hot oak panel. He crawled two more feet and suddenly hit a human leg . . . He fumbled, feeling the cotton of a shirt. It had to be Katie! Throwing aside the jacket, Taylor lunged forward, hooking his hands beneath her armpits. He couldn't see her; the blackness engulfed them. He was barely conscious himself, the smoke stealing his breath, making him weak. No! Don't take her from me. Please don't! He got to his knees and, in a superhuman effort, pulled Katie into his arms and dragged her outside. He was met by several fire fighters who had just appeared around the corner, carrying hoses and breathing apparatus.

Taylor laid Katie on the asphalt, hands splayed near her head. "Get an ambulance! She needs oxygen," he cried. As he looked down at Katie in the shadowy light, his heart shrank in terror; her face was a grayish blue. She had been without oxygen for too long!

Frantically, Taylor placed his fingers on her carotid artery. She had barely any pulse! Quickly one of the fire fighters knelt on her other side and clapped an oxygen mask over her nose and mouth. Taylor gripped her hand, willing his life to flow into her, willing her to live. If she had breathed in enough of that thousand-degree heat to damage her lungs, she'd die anyway. Tears squeezed from his eyes as the fire fighter worked over Katie. Lord, not now. Don't take her away from me. I know I don't deserve her, but please, give me a second chance, please . . .

Chapter **11**

KATIE MOVED SLOWLY through gauzy layers of consciousness, aware of a strong, warm hand holding hers. As she
blinked, her vision cleared, and she saw Taylor and Maud
standing beside her bed. Tears ran down Maud's round
cheeks; her hands were clasped to her breast. Katie's gaze
moved up...up to meet and hold contact with Taylor's
anxious eyes.

"Am I dead?" she croaked.

Maud laughed. A grin stole its way across Taylor's grim
countenance.

"I don't think I'd've made it as an angel," he told Katie
and then glanced at Maud. "Maud might've, but not I."

Katie managed a slight smile, still groggy after hours of
unconsciousness. She squeezed Taylor's hand weakly.

"Don't talk anymore, Katie girl," Maud said, wagging a
finger at her. "You've been out almost five hours. Lord,

girl, you had us worried for a while."

Katie was barely able to raise her lashes. "What?" she said, perplexed.

Taylor gripped her hand more firmly. "The fire, Katie. Remember?" He watched her cloudy blue eyes begin to focus. The doctor had warned them that she might block the whole traumatic episode after regaining consciousness. He had assured them she would remember more as the shock wore off.

"Oh, no . . ."

"It's all right, princess. You're alive and safe. So am I. No one got hurt, thank the Lord."

"That's right, Katie. Look at the bright side: Taylor saved your life by dragging you out of that inferno. The fire chief says you were lucky. Breathing in all that heat and smoke for such a long time! Humph! I told him it wasn't your time to go; you have a lot more to do down here on this old earth of ours."

Slivers of memory, blips of the Molotov cocktail being thrown, the shadowy figure of a man, the explosion, moved like movie frames through her memory. Katie shut her eyes. A deluge of emotion welled up within her, constricting her raw throat. Tears scaled her eyelids. Automatically, she clung tighter to Taylor's hand. "The store," she choked.

Taylor frowned. "Katie, just rest. The doctor said you didn't need to hear—"

Katie forced her eyes open, staring up at him. "Tell me what happened."

He took a deep breath, his heavily bandaged right hand closing over hers. "The bookstore . . . everything is destroyed, princess."

Her eyes widened. "N-not my apartment, too . . . my mother's piano?"

Taylor winced at the pain in her scratchy voice. "Everything. I'm sorry . . ."

No! Katie bit down hard on her lower lip until she tasted blood. She had worked for five years to create that apartment. And her mother's piano . . . the wonderful piano that brought back so many happy childhood memories . . . ashes. Everything gone. Tears slipped from the corners of her eyes, and she felt Taylor brush them away.

"They caught him. The guy who did it," he told her, hoping to erase some of the suffering he saw etched in her face. "He was the first man on my suspect list, the one I saw this morning. After I questioned him, he must have gotten scared." Taylor stroked her ebony hair; it still smelled heavily of smoke. "He's under arrest now. And you're safe."

Maud nudged Taylor sharply, indicating that he should take Katie in his arms. Mouthing the words 'Go on!' the older woman slipped quietly from the room.

A sob tore from Katie's throat as Taylor leaned over the bed, drawing her into his arms.

"Come here, princess. This is our pain, our loss," he said thickly. "I'm responsible for all of this."

"N-no."

"Sshhh, just let me hold you and help you the best I know how. I can't give you back your piano or your apartment, Katie. I know how much they meant to you." Taylor kissed her damp temple, burying his face in her hair. "All you have left is a jaded big-city reporter in the clutches of a premature midlife crisis. But I'll be here for you, Katie, if you'll let me. I'll help you rebuild, or do anything you want."

She clung to him, needing his love and the unsteady words that tore from deep within him. "Y-you're not jaded," she managed. "And I don't blame you for what happened."

Taylor eased her back so that he could look into tear-filled eyes that were little more than wounded holes of grief. "I love you, Katie. My love can't replace what you lost, but maybe, if you want it to, it can give you the strength to carry on."

Her heart mushroomed with such violent joy that Katie thought she might die. The euphoria flowed through her as she met his dark gray eyes, glittering dangerously with tears. "You love me? You really do?"

He managed a shaky laugh. "Yeah. Why are you looking at me so strangely? It's not a joke, princess. And I'm not saying it out of guilt, either." He cradled her face between his hands. "I almost lost you, Katie. I was beside myself when I couldn't find you in the apartment." He shut his eyes. "As I ran back down the stairs, I knew I couldn't picture life without you. Without your laughter, your special way of looking at things. I stopped believing in God a long time ago, back when I was working the crime beat. At least I thought I did. When I was running around the back of the bookstore, trying to gain entrance, I prayed, Katie. I told God if he'd give me a second chance and let me find you alive, I'd try to straighten out my life, my priorities." He opened stormy gray eyes to hold hers. "It's not important at the moment whether you . . . love me or not. I'm older and more experienced. When you came crashing into my life, you changed everything." He managed a smile. "I just didn't want to admit it at first. But the fire, and almost losing you, changed everything."

Katie reached up to touch his charcoal-smudged cheek. She wasn't sure who smelled more of smoke or looked more disheveled. "Can I go home with you, Taylor? Do I have to stay here tonight?"

He leaned down, tenderly caressing her lips. "You have to stay overnight for observation. How about if I come by tomorrow morning and pick you up? The doctor said you should be ready for release by then."

So much was happening! Katie nodded, unable to separate her joy from her loss. She tilted her head, pressing her lips to his mouth, reveling in being alive, being loved.

Tomorrow would come soon enough. And with it, she would see the destruction that the fire had wrought . . .

Taylor had brought a pair of his beige chino pants and a light blue sport shirt for Katie to wear. Her face was pale as he walked her out of the hospital and to the Trans Am. The bright California sunshine streamed down, and Katie absorbed the rays like a starved winter flower. Right now, Taylor's strength was her strength. After he had left last night, she had cried herself to sleep. But she woke up now and then, reliving the horror of the fire. The dark circles under her eyes looked permanent as she stared in the mirror this morning. She didn't look like the vivacious Katie who flitted like a butterfly through life's trials and crises . . .

She hugged her arms around herself. Taylor glanced her way as they drove from the hospital.

"Cold?"

"No. I was just thinking."

"About what?"

Her mouth tilted painfully. "How old I feel. I don't feel like myself, Taylor. It's frightening."

He placed his arm around her shoulder, drawing her close. "It's the shock. Nothing more."

Katie rallied. "Are you sure? I feel so empty inside. As if I'm dead or something."

"Trust me. I've seen plenty of victims traumatized by burglary, physical assault, rape, and anything other crime you care to name, Katie. They all react the same way: They have that desolate, hollow feeling inside."

"Does it go away?"

"Eventually," Taylor promised. "Sooner for some, later for others." Taylor smiled over at her. Katie looked fragile, and that scared him. He'd never seen her melancholy; he was used to her vibrant smile and those beautiful lapis eyes shining with the warmth of the sun. But didn't everyone have vulnerable areas? His broken marriage had been his.

Katie's loss of her source of income and her home was even more severe a blow. Taylor hated to talk business, but he knew they had to.

"Katie, was your bookstore insured?"

She looked away, staring blindly out the window. "I couldn't afford to pay insurance premiums, Taylor. I barely made the mortgage payment every month. I knew I should have coverage, but I just didn't have the money. I lost at least fifty thousand dollars' worth of books in that fire. I owe another twenty thousand on the building so I guess the bank will take the property and the building insurance." Katie rubbed her forehead, willing away the tears that wanted to fall.

"How about your apartment? The piano?"

Pain ripped through her. "No," she whispered rawly, "nothing was insured."

"I see." He wished he could shelter Katie from the shock of seeing the gutted building. Taylor felt helpless as he guided the growling Trans Am around the corner and down the street toward the spot where her bookstore had been. "There's not much left to see, princess." He braked and parked, glancing over at Katie. Her eyes were huge, and the remaining color had drained from her face. Dammit, he could do nothing to ease her anguish. He got out and opened her door, helping her out.

Kaite was determined not to cry. Among the crowd on the street she recognized at least a dozen of her aging friends, people who had brought their pets to her in the past. Dr. Abrams and his red-haired wife Toni stood solemnly with them. They waited on her in a semicircle. Maud was with them, her face set and resolute. Behind them was a burned-out brick shell that had once been Katie's entire world. Now it was nothing more than a few charred timbers here and there, scattered like toothpicks by some unseen giant hand, and ashes almost a foot deep everywhere else. Even now, the debris smoldered, white wisps of smoke rising here and there from the ruins.

Taylor put his arm around Katie, drawing her close. He looked down at her, his eyes tender. "There're an awful lot of people who love you, Katie. They've been waiting most of the morning here for you."

Katie tried to smile as Taylor drew her to a halt. He released her, and the small crowd enclosed her. Proud, thin Mrs. Beaumont, who lived off a meager fixed income that hugged the poverty level, was the first to embrace her.

"Now, you just dry those tears, Katie," the old woman whispered fiercely, holding Katie with all the failing strength of her eighty-nine-year-old arms. "We got all the neighbors together last night after Mr. Grant told us you were going to be fine." She smiled and stepped back, her green eyes watering. Digging into her crocheted handbag, she pulled out a check, waving it under Katie's nose.

"I went around last night and told everyone about what had happened to you. All of us who had ever come to you for help donated money to help you build another bookstore, Katie." Mrs. Beaumont pushed the check into Katie's hand. "Here, you take this. It isn't much, but it's a start. As we've already told Maud, we're all prepared to help. Why, I'm a whiz when it comes to painting. And Mrs. Talbot says she'll hang wallpaper. And grumpy old Mr. Evans has promised to do some carpentering for you."

Tears blurred Katie's vision as she looked down at the neatly typed cashier's check from a local bank: $952.56. A sob caught in her aching throat. Most of her patients were elderly and lived on fixed incomes. They couldn't afford to give this kind of money to anyone. More, how could she tell all these wonderful people that their generous gift was a mere drop in the bucket, compared to the thousands she now owed.

"Oh . . . Mrs. Beaumont—"

"Don't you *dare* try to give that back, young lady!" Mrs. Beaumont warned archly, taking a step back, her chin held high.

"But—"

Taylor stepped to her side, realizing Katie wasn't able to cope with the situation. He put an arm around her and smiled at Mrs. Beaumont.

"I just want all of you to know that Claire Garvey of the Raintree Restaurant has invited anyone who donated to Katie's new bookstore down for afternoon tea at four o'clock this afternoon. Can you all make it? Mrs. Beaumont, can you spread the word? I'll arrange transportation for those who need it."

Katie raised her head to give Taylor a blank look. Tears streamed down her cheeks as she clutched the check in her hand.

With a pert nod, Mrs. Beaumont tapped her cane smartly on the sidewalk. "Wonderful, Mr. Grant! I'll accept Mrs. Garvey's kind invitation on behalf of everyone concerned."

Confused, Katie hugged each and every individual, voicing her thanks. And when Dr. Abrams and his wife came over, giving Taylor a knowing grin, she was even more confused.

"We'll see you this afternoon, Katie," Dr. Abrams told her, patting her hand.

She and Taylor were left standing alone near the gutted building. Katie looked at it; there wasn't a shred of evidence that her mother's piano had ever existed. Nothing survived. She looked down at the check and then over at Taylor.

"I-I never expected this. Look at the amount. None of them can afford this, Taylor."

He smiled, looking deeply into her beautiful blue eyes. "They gave from their hearts, Katie. Aren't you the one who always said that gifts from the heart are the richest kind? That money pales in comparison? Well, that's how they felt about helping you get back on your feet." He took her arm, gently pulling her from the once-beautiful apartment and the crazy little bookstore. "Come on, princess, we've got to get you some new clothes. You can't go to tea looking like a bedraggled puppy, now can you?"

The Raintree Restaurant was filled to capacity; over one hundred fifty people were seated when Taylor and Katie arrived. She hung close to him, feeling emotional and out of balance from the whirlwind pace of the day. When she stepped through the revolving glass and brass door, the entire restaurant crowd broke into welcoming applause. Claire Garvey came forward, a huge smile on her face as she pulled Katie to her side. Taylor remained discreetly in the background, hands in the pockets of his dark brown slacks, a tender smile pulling at the corners of his mouth.

"Katie, we just want you to know," Claire began, her strong voice carrying over the assemblage, "we're glad to have you with us." She tucked her arm around Katie's waist, drawing her toward the center of the restaurant. Katie recognized almost every business owner in Rio Conchos. More important, all her elderly friends were there, too, smiling broadly, their eyes shining. And down in front, with Suzie in her cage, sat little Brandon Prater and his parents, Scott and Jo Ann. Katie gave Claire a helpless look.

"Claire, what's going on here?"

The crowd erupted into delighted laughter.

Claire grinned. "We're glad you asked that, Katie. Now, you just stand here while I go through this speech I prepared especially of you. From all of us. There isn't one person in this room who can remember a time when you didn't give us a smile, a cheerful word, a quick hug, or, most important, your wonderful touch when we needed it. When word spread about how you'd been harassed by telephone for three terrible weeks and our police department did little to try to apprehend the caller, we all felt guilty, Katie. You always gave without asking for anything in return. And before you open your mouth, we all know how you feel on that subject!"

Laughter filled the room.

Claire smiled. "We know you believe in something called the cosmos and karma. You never charged a penny for your services, not to touch an ailing pet or to touch us when we had an aching shoulder, a severe headache, or worse. You wouldn't let anyone pay you for gas to take people shopping or on errands." Her smile disappeared. "Well, Katie, we know you lost everything. And we want you to stay in Rio Conchos and build us another bookstore, a place where we can bring our pets—and ourselves, too."

Katie shot a glance at Taylor who was leaning casually against the wall, his eyes burning with a fierce tenderness. She swallowed painfully. "I-I don't understand, Claire. You've already given me a check for a lot of money."

Claire patted her hand in motherly fashion. "Just stand here and listen for the next fifteen minutes, Katie, and you'll see."

The mayor of Rio Conchos, Ben McCord, who was also president of the bank where Katie took out her loan and the owner of a huge lumberyard, stood up. He was a rotund man, and he straightened his loosely fitting sports coat.

"Katie, as a private citizen of Rio Conchos," he began in his best political stumping voice, "it's my honor to donate the lumber for your new bookshop. As a businessman and president of the bank, I've decided to let your loan float until your store is built." His joviality dissolved. "And as mayor of this fine California community, I apologize on behalf of our police department. Changes are being made to ensure that every citizen is equally protected under the law."

Dick Martin, owner of the hardware store, stood up next. "Katie, we'd be honored if you'd take whatever items you need to hang those boards together with." A round of laughter. "Don Mayer? You own a construction outfit. What have you donated to help Katie get back on her feet?"

Stunned by the outpouring of generosity, Katie could only stand, gripping Claire's hand. This wasn't a dream! Each person who donated goods or services was earnest and sincere. By the time they were done, Katie was dazed.

"Now, all these fine people have donated the materials for your new bookstore, Katie," Claire said. "But one thing is missing. A building lot!"

Everyone laughed.

"Taylor Grant?" Claire called.

Katie looked toward him as he slowly walked to the spot where she and Claire stood. He was wearing that same odd smile, and her heart beat a little harder to underscore the intensity of her emotions. Katie swallowed her tears as Taylor came to her side. He smiled and then looked over the hushed, expectant audience, picking up Katie's hands in his.

"Normally, I'm not one who likes being in the spotlight," he began awkwardly. His voice grew stronger as he continued. "Most of you know by now of the blunder I made. I did a story on Katie that more or less called her a fake. It started a messy chain of events that ended nearly taking her life." Taylor looked down at her, his voice strained. "I'm the one who took away her bookstore and her world. I may never be able to replace what she lost, but I'd like to try to atone by donating the land for her next bookstore." He cleared his throat. "How does a corner lot in the Rancho Santa Fe mall sounds to you, Katie?"

Surprise widened her eyes. "Rancho Santa Fe?" she squeaked. "But that's the busiest mall in the county! And store space runs—"

"I just signed a two year lease on behalf of the Unicorn Bookstore. The lot is located on the busiest corner in the mall."

My God! Katie opened her mouth and then shut it. How could Taylor have gotten that kind of money? He wasn't rich! And then a wave of anxiety hit her: Had the crazy, wonderful idiot sold his car and his house or gone into hock up to his elbows to get that lease? She was vaguely aware of the crowd coming to its feet and applause thundering through the restaurant. She stared blankly up at Taylor, the question "how?" implicit in her gaze. A boyish smile crossed his mouth, and he leaned over, lips near her ear.

"I sold some blue-chip stocks I was saving for a rainy day. Now, stop worrying, Katie. I didn't sell my soul to the devil to get that lease for you. Okay?"

The stars hung huge and close, like small crystals suspended by some unseen hand in the black velvet of the heavens. Katie sighed as she stood on the back porch of Taylor's home, a pale pink shawl across her shoulders. She turned when she heard his footsteps.

"There you are."

Katie smiled as he halted behind her and drew her to him, wrapping his arms around her, holding her close. "I just can't believe today, Taylor. It's like a dream."

"One that came true for a fairy-tale princess who believes in miracles." He inhaled the lilac scent of her skin, finding the nape of her neck, kissing her gently.

"I'm so tired, and yet I'm so excited and humbled and grateful and—"

"Loved."

She closed her eyes, relaxing completely in his embrace. "I never knew how much until today," she admitted softly. And then Katie stared up at his dark, shadowy face. A fierce need welled up within her.

"I've come to the conclusion you're a butterfly reincarnated into human form, Katie Riordan," Taylor whispered huskily. "How can I keep a butterfly captive when I know it should fly free?"

Katie heard the underlying worry in his tone and turned in his arms. "You don't know?"

His eyes were dark, and he shook his head, bleakness in his voice. "No . . . I wish I did."

She stretched up on tiptoe, pressing her lips to his mouth. "It's easy: If the butterfly comes back to you, then it's yours to keep." She molded herself to him, feeling him tense. "I've come home, Taylor. You're my home, my freedom . . ." And she kissed him as though she would never kiss him again.

He shuddered, then embraced Katie, hardly daring to believe what he had heard. He pressed his face against hers. "Lord, we've come through so much in such a short time, Katie. But I feel as though I've known you forever." His arms tightened around her, and he savored her lilting laugh.

"I believe in reincarnation," she confided, holding him tightly, kissing him along the hard line of his jaw. "The moment you came to help me pick up my books, I thought, Where have you been? I've been waiting for you all my life." She sighed, content as never before. "You've helped me through so much, Taylor."

He arched a brow. "I? Helped you?"

Katie nodded soberly. "Did Mary Ann tell you that you never helped anyone? That all you could do was destroy and tear things apart?"

Taylor nodded. Gently he lifted her in his arms and carried her inside the house and to his bedroom. It was a spare bedroom in dire need of a woman's touch. "That was pretty much it," he admitted, setting Katie on the bed and lying down beside her.

"Don't ever believe that again, Taylor. Without you, I

couldn't have survived this, and I know it." Katie shrugged. "You're right. I am a butterfly. No one is more aware of my strengths and weaknesses than I. I know I can't take a lot of stress. You can. I don't know how to defend myself." She sat up, holding his bandaged hand between hers. "Some people were put on this earth to help. Others to do different jobs. All of us are important. You've been my strength, my beautiful dark knight with the heart of a unicorn. You've sustained me. I'd've fallen apart after the fire if you hadn't been there." Her left hand grew hot, and she smiled tenderly at Taylor, who had an odd look on his face.

"This is all I do well, darling. It's one form of healing. You've healed me in other ways."

Taylor felt the frantic tingling sensation move across his badly blistered palm, which was swathed in gauze. This was his Katie. "You've healed my heart, too, princess."

She leaned over, and her mouth met his. Glorying in the strength of his returning ardor, she whispered, "I love you."

"Enough to marry me?"

"Yes."

"And have kids—who I'm sure will be real hellions, because I was one myself?"

She smiled against his mouth, running her tongue delicately across his lower lip, feeling him tense. His good hand slid up her rib cage to caress her breast. "Yes," she breathed, lifting her hands and framing his face. "I want a hundred of them."

"My income won't cover that many. Will you settle on three or four little unicorns instead?"

With a soft laugh, Katie slid down beside him, her eyes lustrous with love for him. "Knowing a Scorpio's capacity for passion, we'll end up with half a dozen."

He grinned, easing her back on the bed, thinking how incredibly beautiful she looked in her loose cotton print dress, splashed with a rainbow of colors. He tunneled his fingers through her thick, soft hair, marveling at its silky curls, a grin hovering on his face. "Scorpios are just very loving," he corrected, nibbling at her earlobe and then trailing a path of kisses down her slender neck. "And I'm going to enjoy every flight of the unicorn with you, my lovely princess . . . forever."

SECOND CHANCE AT LOVE

COMING NEXT MONTH

HEAVEN CAN WAIT #364 by Dianne Thomas
Brandon Wilder can't get past first base with softball
coach and responsible mother Kelly O'Brien—until he
suggests a weekend affair. With no strings attached,
what could go wrong? Plenty!

CONQUER THE NIGHT #365 by Karen Keast
Bent on violence to avenge a vicious crime,
hardened detective Laird Roberts brusquely denies
needing psychologist detective Charley Ware.
Yet his bluntly sensual tactics clearly prove he *wants* her...

SUN-KISSED HEARTS #366 by Kit Windham
Virile, dashing Gib Maclaren: In five years, she
hasn't forgotten him. She'll *never* forgive him. Sweet,
sexy Beth Faraday: He's never stopped loving
her. He'll stop at nothing to claim her!

SWEET TEMPTATION #367 by Diana Mars
Earthy biologist Fletcher Tierney tempts coolly
scientific Luna Flyer into revealing her sensual, fun-loving
side...enticing her into one wickedly indiscreet
situation after another...demolishing her self-control!

TWICE IN A LIFETIME #368 by Pat Dalton
Kelly's last whirlwind passion ended painfully when
Linc left on a simple errand—and never returned! Now,
years later, she's afraid to love Chase Granger, who
bears an uncanny resemblance to the devastating Linc...

CREATURE COMFORTS #369 by Adrienne Edwards
Amanda MacGee's summer plans go awry when
self-proclaimed artist, poet, and lover extraordinaire
Richard O'Brien blithely moves in—then recruits
even her dog and cat in an all-out campaign
to charm and seduce her!

SECOND CHANCE AT LOVE

Be Sure to Read These New Releases!

BEST OF STRANGERS #352 by Courtney Ryan
As one comically disastrous encounter follows another,
Jenny Shapiro and Tony Coulter agree they've got to stop
meeting like this. But catastrophe is beginning to feel
normal...and being together as natural as love!

WHISPERS FROM THE PAST #353 by Mary Haskell
Powerfully attracted despite their opposing
claims to a spooky old house, Vicki Addison and
Mark Rogers sense the mysterious echoes, and
inexplicable pull, of a love that may be centuries old...

POCKETFUL OF MIRACLES #354 by Diana Morgan
Burned out and confused, Mallory Taylor hops
a ferry to Nantucket and embarks on an adventurous
new life—complete with roguishly lovable, forgivably
overbearing, irresistibly appealing "Mac" McClintock.

**RECKLESS GLANCES, STOLEN CHANCES #355
by Lee Williams**
When Claudia Wells inadvertently agrees to a
handsome stranger's crazy, tantalizing proposition,
she becomes embroiled in a fraud-filled caper and
thrilling romantic entanglement of devastating proportions!

BY LOVE BETRAYED #356 by Ada John
Hired under false pretenses, Lainie Wilson
acts as companion to the teenage daughter of reclusive,
autocratic Paul Reynard—then must divide her
loyalties as she confronts the masterfully sexy Frenchman.

LONG ROAD HOME #357 by Jean Fauré
Truck driver Erin Taliferro reluctantly accepts
brawny Luke Reardon's offer of help. But his disturbing
reticence...and the exquisite tension of their
enforced intimacy...drive her into an emotional tailspin!

Order on opposite page